Your Cheatin' Heart

★

Written and Illustrated by
John Byrne

★

BBC BOOKS

The 6-part series *Your Cheatin' Heart* was produced
by BBC Scotland and first shown on BBC 1 in October 1990.

Executive Producer Bill Bryden
Musical Directors Robert Noakes and Michael Marra
Film Editor John MacDonnell
Photography Garry Morrison
Designer Bob Smart
Director Michael Whyte
Producer Peter Broughan

Published by BBC Books,
A division of BBC Enterprises Limited,
Woodlands, 80 Wood Lane, London W12 0TT

First published 1990
© John Byrne 1990
ISBN 0 563 36049 6

Set in 12/15pt Palatino by Goodfellow & Egan Ltd, Cambridge
Printed and bound in England by Richard Clay Ltd, St Ives Plc, Bungay
Cover printed by Richard Clay Ltd, St Ives Plc, Norwich

Contents

Cast List

Cissie Crouch .... *Tilda Swinton*

Frank McClusky .... *John Gordon Sinclair*

Fraser Boyle .... *Ken Stott*

Dorwood Crouch .... *Kevin McMonagle*

David Cole .... *Guy Gregory*

Billie McPhail .... *Katy Murphy*

Jolene Jowett .... *Eddi Reader*

Shirley .... *Barbara Rafferty*

Tracey .... *Jenny McCrindle*

Diner in the Bar-L .... *Troy Fairclough*

Young Woman in Bar-L Ladies' Room .... *Fenella Kerr*

Spencer the barman .... *Leo Sho Silva*

Timberwolf Tierney (Aka the Tall Cowpoke) .... *Tom Watson*

Cherokee George .... *Tom Watson*

Policeman at roadblock .... *David Gallagher*

MC at Ponderosa .... *Fred Brodie*

Libo Ragazzo .... *Richard Jobson*

Secretary .... *Daniela Nardini*

Young man outside the Bar-L .... *Troy Fairclough*

Girlfriend outside the Bar-L .... *Maureen Japp*

Milkman .... *Robbie Shepherd*

Police Constable .... *Michael Reilly*

The Toad .... *Freddie Boardley*

First Patrol Officer .... *James MacDonald*

Second Patrol Officer .... *David Meldrum*

Newsreader on TV .... *Cathy MacDonald*

Jim Bob O'May .... *Guy Mitchell*

Jonathan Ross as Himself

1

Throwing Up in the Gorbals

Glasgow, at dusk. A ghostly sickle moon scythes its way between the dark rain clouds that hang over HM prison Barlinnie, (known affectionately to Glaswegians by its 'Cowboy' nickname, the 'Bar-L').

In the visiting room of the prison Cissie Crouch, beanpole-skinny and wearing a dark grey and white horizontally-striped suit buttoned to the throat and with a number tag stitched to the breast pocket, sits across the visiting room table from her husband Dorwood. His features are pale, impassive. He is dressed in jeans and an unshowy cowboy shirt, his hair neatly groomed.

The atmosphere in the room is tense, as one might expect.

A female prison officer, hands folded behind her back, stands at a not-quite-discreet-enough distance from the couple.

Neither Cissie nor Dorwood speaks to the other.

Cissie reaches a tentative hand across the table. Dorwood draws his hands away.

A distant bell sounds.

Dorwood scrapes back his chair and stands up. The female prison officer crosses and unlocks a door. Dorwood pulls on his denim jacket and moves to the door.

Cissie] Dorwood?

Cissie half-rises in her seat. Dorwood reaches the door, stops, and turns.

Dorwood] The suit isnae funny, Cissie.

Cissie's face falls.

A male prison officer appears in the doorway, takes Dorwood by the arm and leads him out.

The female officer hands Cissie her bag.

We hear the men's footsteps fade off down the corridor.

13

Cissie crosses to the door, and emerges from the visiting room into the corridor as Dorwood is being escorted back to his cell, her face distorted into an angry mask.

Cissie [*Loudly*] If you weren't in here I wouldnae have to wear this funny suit!

★　★　★

The 'Bar-L' is Glasgow's newest piano bar and grill. It is evening, and the ziggurat neon sign flashes in the dark.
　　Inside Cissie is taking down a banquette's order in her pad.

Cissie] Yeh, the specials are really nice . . . would you care for some cornbread with that?

The Bar-L is not a 'fun pub', but a straight eatery set out along New York lines: baby-grand surrounded by bar stools at one end of the room, semi-circular banquettes around the walls, and a bar for cocktails, dining, and serious posing.

14

*The one concession to frivolity
(aside from the establishment's name)
is the waiting staff's livery: the two
other waitresses, Tracey and Shirley,
are, like Cissie, togged out in
modishly-cut 'convict' trouser suits.*

*David Cole, the black American
manager, immaculate in white tux,
sits at the piano, his fingers caressing
a medley of 40s' hits from the
keyboard.*

*Spencer, the barman, spends his
afternoons at the movies and is a big
Tom Cruise fan.*

Cissie crosses to the bar.

Cissie] Give us a Margherita, will
you?

*Spencer displays the enviable
dexterity of a juggler as he handles
the order.*

*Cissie turns round, rests her
elbows on the bartop, and
lets out an exhausted sigh.*

David Cole] Hey, you.

*Cissie looks around,
wondering who it is
he's talking to.*

David Cole] Yeah, you . . .
Jessie.
Cissie] Cissie.
David Cole] C'mere.

Cissie crosses to the piano.

Cissie] What?

David Cole carries on playing.

David Cole] How long you been
workin' here?

Cissie's lip curls.

TRACEY   SHIRLEY

15

Cissie] What's this, a variation on 'How many fingers am I holdin' up?' I told you when I started, I never touch the stuff . . . that cocktail's for a customer.

Cole's mood darkens.

David Cole] Hey, don't get sassy with me, Red . . . five days awready, an' nobody's seen you crack a smile.

He segues into Billy Joel's 'Just the Way You Are'.

Cissie] So, what you tellin' me?
David Cole] Lighten up or take a hike, that's what I'm tellin' you.

Cissie touches a forelock and tries to turn the contemptuous twist of her mouth to a smile.

It's night-time, and on a gap-site in a rundown part of the city there is an eruption of crackling on a two-way radio, the single intelligible word of which is an 'over' at the end.

Frank] I'm positive it's about here someplace.

Billie McPhail is standing by her taxi. She is wearing a New York Police Department leather jacket, baggy trousers, and short cowboy boots. She reaches into the cab and unhooks the mike.

Billie [*On radio*] Car Fourteen, say again, over?

Frank McClusky, your quintessential 'new' Glaswegian, is standing a few yards distant, with the toecaps of his stout brogues submerged in a scummy cesspool, and his eyes peering into the gloom of the 'bombsite'.
    Frank is dressed in an enormous Burberry, belted but unbuttoned so that it flaps decorously around the turnups of his Harris Tweed pegbottoms. His shirt is a Japanese/ French co-production retailing at around £150 and looking like it's been slept in more than once.

Frank] It's a low-rise buildin' with a pokey hat on the roof.

He paces across the rubble-strewn wasteland.

Billie] With a what on the roof?

Frank scrapes the sole of his shoe along the ground and wishes a pox on all dog-owners.

Frank] A pokey hat. Used to be Ragazzo's ice-cream works.

There is a short eruption of static over the radio.

Billie [*On radio*] Naw, I cannae, Jolene. I'm stuck out here in the middle of the Okeyfenokey Swamp

with a boy scout in a belltent lookin' for a low-rise buildin' with a pokey hat on the roof. Give Car Twenty-Six a shout, over.

There is another short burst on the radio.

Billie [*On radio*] Naw, a pokey hat, over. (*To Frank*) Don't tell me you've spent . . .

She glances at the meter. The fare is £8.

Billie] . . . just to come out here an' buy yourself a wafer? We musta passed umpteen ice-cream vans on the road in.

Frank] Used to be, I said . . . it's now a very snazzy piano bar and grill specialisin' in Soul Food. Wish to Christ I could remember the name of it . . .

He stares up at the stars.

Billie] You're not the only one. [*On radio*] Car Fourteen, you there, Jolene, over?

Frank] Flang its portals open to the cognoscenti last Monday night . . .

There is a short burst on the radio.

Billie [*On radio*] Yeh, piano bar an' grill specialisin' in Soul Food, Duke Street area, over?

Frank] I was away coverin' a

clambake in Seamill which is how come I missed the launch . . .

There's another short burst on the radio.

Billie [*On radio*] Naw . . . Soul . . . guy says you have to get a boat out to it, over.

Frank wanders off across the 'bombsite'.

Frank] You mebbe read my piece in the *Echo*?
Billie] *Echo*?
Frank] *Echo*.

Another eruption of static on the radio.

Frank] My piece about the clambake, naw?
Billie [*On radio*] Hold on, I'll ask. [*To Frank*] Jolene wants to know is it The Clappy Doo in Clyde Street? She's got that in her yella pages under 'Sole, Haddock & Whiting'.

Frank fixes Billie with a bilious stare.

Back in the Bar-L Shirley and Tracey are in a huddle behind the kitchen door marked 'out'.
As Cissie enters the 'in' door, Tracey hides a copy of the Glasgow Evening Echo *behind her back.*

Cissie [*Loudly*] Four Claws, two Grits, one Gumbo.

Cissie turns to go, gives Shirley and Tracey a look, then leaves.
Shirley makes a grab for Tracey's tabloid.

Shirley] Quick, give us a look.
Tracey] Stop crowdin' us . . .

She opens the paper and finds a big publicity picture of the Deadwood Playboys, Dorwood Crouch, Fraser Boyle, and Dwane Devlin, onstage in colour, together with a grainy black and white photograph of Dorwood and Dwane being led handcuffed from court under a banner headline: 'DEADWOOD DUO'S SHAME AS SHERIFF CRACKS DOWN ON COWBOY COKEHEADS'.

Shirley [*Reading*] 'Dwane & Dorwood Hit Trail to Pokey ! . . . In Clydebank Hold-Up Trial' . . .

Her brows knit. She looks at Tracey.

. . . Pokey? Like in hat, naw?
Tracey] Pokey, like in prison, ya dope . . . they got put away for nine years.
Shirley] Aaah, that's how come the face is trippin' her? S'that him there?

She points at the paper.

Tracey] Naw, that's Dwane . . . Listen to this . . . [*Reads*] 'Thirty-four-year-old Crouch, speaking for the first time during the two-day trial, said that he and fellow "Playboy", Dwane Devlin, forty-two, were "poleaxed" when police stopped Devlin's Fiesta in Faifley and found . . .'

Shirley [*Interrupting*] You ever dined out in Faifley? I wouldn't recommend it. Carry on.

Tracey [*Reads*] '. . . and found a quantity of cocaine and a hammer, later identified as the one used in the Post Office raids, concealed inside a pair of brand-new size 10½ cowboy boots on the back seat. Giving evidence, DC Douglas Weir of Strathclyde Serious Crime Squad, said that when challenged, the Clydebank-based Country singer said . . .'

Shirley [*Interjecting*] Aw, look, he's quite nice.

She leans close to paper.

Tracey] '. . . Yes, they are mine but I have never seen those dot dot drugs or that dot dot hammer in my . . .' Where? Get your noddle out the road.

Another article on the same page has the headline 'PISMO CLAMS "HIT THE SPOT" IN SEAMILL'. It carries

the byline 'Rab Haw', (a corruption of the name 'Robert Hall', the legendary nineteenth-century 'Glasgow Glutton', who is said to have consumed four cows, two sheep, and forty-four black puddings at one sitting), together with a head-shot of Frank McClusky.

Shirley] Not him . . . him there.

Shirley points to the Deadwood Playboys' picture where Fraser Boyle is flanked by Dwane and Dorwood, overstamped in red with '2 yrs' and '7 yrs' respectively.

Tracey] What . . . him in the middle? He didnae even get indicted, Shirley.

Shirley] You don't have to get indicted to qualify as a hunk,

Tracey] It says here he sells fish . . . what's got into you?

She looks askance at Shirley.

Shirley] Shut your mug . . . what does it say about *her*?

Tracey] *Her* who?

Shirley] Look out.

Cissie re-enters the kitchen.

Cissie [*Loudly*] Five Chitlin', one Baby Ribs, one Chilliburger!

Tracey stuffs the newspaper inside her jacket.

Shirley [*To Cissie*] If you need a hand out there just . . .

Cissie sweeps out again.

Shirley . . . give us a shout. [*To Tracey*]
Her . . . I want to hear what it says about . . .

Cissie's head reappears round the door.

Cissie] Sorry to disappoint you, girls, but it doesn't say anythin' about *her* 'cos *her* refused to talk to that rag, right?

Her head disappears again.
   Shirley looks at Tracey, and Tracey looks away.

In another part of the city on an abandoned factory site Billie perches on the taxi wing, mike in hand, while Frank prowls around the 'ghost town'.

Billie [*On radio*] See when you're comin', Jolene, gonnae bring all my stuff over, over?

There is a garbled response over the radio.

Billie [*On radio*] 'Cos I'm never gonnae get back in time to get changed, this galoot's got us drivin' all over, over.

Another longer incoherent eruption over the radio.

Billie [*On radio*] Naw, they're in gettin' soled an' heeled, the ones I wore to the Cowdenbeath Rodeo with the frogs on them, over.

By now Frank has fallen into conversation with a filthy-looking individual in ragged topcoat and matted hair. Money changes hands between them.

Billie] Aw, brilliant . . . if you want to know where the nearest snazzy Soul Food bar is, ask your friendly neighbourhood wino.

She hooks the mike back up inside the cab.

Billie [*Loudly*] This meter's still runnin'!

While Billie resticks her collection of Patsy Cline cut-outs on to the glass partition Frank parts company with the derelict and makes his way back to the taxi.

Frank] Bumped into an old school chum.

He replaces his now empty wallet in his hip pocket.

Billie] Yeh . . . 'gaudeamus igitur' . . . gonnae just gimme the fare an' I'll blow? Me an' Jolene's

20

got a gig at the Cactus Club at half
ten.

Frank] Dropped outta dental college,
he was tellin' me.

*Billie glances at the meter as Frank
delves into his Burberry pocket and
brings out a crumpled newspaper
'poke' full of blackened shellfish.*

Billie] Call it fifteen quid, okay?

*Frank is picking through the scorched
seafood, discarding the obviously
untouchable bits.*

Frank [*Shocked*] Fifteen quid?

Billie] Cash . . . we stopped takin'
cowrie shells back in '49.

Frank] You get any funnier an' we'll
get you a balloon on a stick . . .
this's my doggy-bag from the
Clambake . . .

*He takes a pin from his lapel and
prises a particularly unappetising-
looking wulk from its shell.*

Billie] An' I'm supposed to stand
here an' watch you eatin' it? Fifteen
quid . . . hurry up.

Frank] I don't want to purchase the
heap, sweetheart . . .

He pops the wulk into his mouth.

Frank] Besides, I've already got
myself a motor . . .

He cracks open a disgusting mussel.

Frank] You ever had a hurl in the
front seat of a white T-bird?

Billie] Naw, an' unless you cough up
pronto you're for a doin' in the
back seat of a Black Maria. Fifteen
quid, cash . . . c'mon!

*A battered delivery van with a faded
fishmonger's name on the side draws
up outside the Bar-L and the driver
climbs out.*

*Fraser Boyle is a muscular man in
his middle thirties with a bruiser's
'handsome' features. He is dressed in
an interesting mix of old-style 'trail-
wear' and 'new wave' Western gear, a
pair of well-worn, highly ornamented
cowboy boots on his feet.*

*Boyle looks up at the Bar-L sign,
dons a pair of leather gloves, and
slams the van door.*

*Inside the bar Cissie is serving
drinks to a banquette, and she glances
up as Boyle enters from the street.*

Diner] Aaargh . . . what you givin'
us!

*Cissie has just served a plate of
Crawdaddy Claws in the diner's lap.*

Cissie] What you ordered. Here.

She chucks a napkin at the disgruntled diner and beats a retreat in the direction of the rest rooms.

Shirley [*To Tracey*] Lemme see that newspaper a minute.

David Cole breaks off after sharing a joke with customers.

David Cole] Enjoy yourselves, huh?

He slides off the banquette and crosses to the door where Boyle is chewing gum and rubber-necking.

Cissie enters the ladies powder room and leans her back against the door, her fists clenched.
A young woman, repairing lipstick in the mirror, pouts in Cissie's direction.

Young Woman] Long're you in for?
Cissie [*Preoccupied*] What?
Young Woman] The outfit . . . it's cute.

Back in the bar David Cole speaks to Fraser Boyle.

David Cole] I think you maybe lost your way, man . . .

He takes Boyle's elbow.

Boyle] I've came about the fish.

He disengages Cole's hand from his elbow.

David Cole] Fish? What you talkin' 'bout, fish?
Boyle] Red snapper, blue snapper, conger eel, turbot . . .

Boyle heads towards a corner banquette.

Boyle] . . . angel fish, queenies, lobster, wulks . . .
David Cole] Sure, sure . . . lemme redirect you to the street, huh?

He catches up with Boyle and takes a firm grip of his arm.

Boyle] You werenae listenin', big boy . . .

Again he prises Cole's fingers from hs sleeve.

Boyle] . . . like, I've been sent to take your 'order', yeh?

He plonks himself down in the corner banquette.
Shirley approaches.

Shirley] Hi, there . . .

She gives Boyle a big smile and sets a glass of iced water down in front of him.

Shirley] What can I get you, Mr Cole?

David Cole] Later, honey . . .

Boyle] I'll've pinta lager, gorgeous.

David Cole] Give 'im a beer.
[*To Boyle*] Listen, punk, I don't know who the hell you are but . . .

Shirley [*Interrupting*] Will that be lite, ultra-lite, root, or regular?

She bares her teeth at Boyle in what she imagines to be a sexy grin.

David Cole] Jus' give 'im a goddam beer, Shelley!

Shirley] Shirley. Sure.

She smiles over her shoulder at Boyle and sashays off to the bar, tray held high. Boyle's eyes follow her.

David Cole] Awright, so what's with the fish, huh?

Boyle] Relax, man . . . I'm to be your go-between . . .

He turns to face Cole.

Boyle] . . . meetin's set up for the morra.

He takes a pencil stub from his ear and a grubby order pad from his jacket pocket.

Boyle [*Loudly*] So, that's four box of flounder, five box of haddie, an' six dozen lobster . . . D'you want the lobster humanely put down?

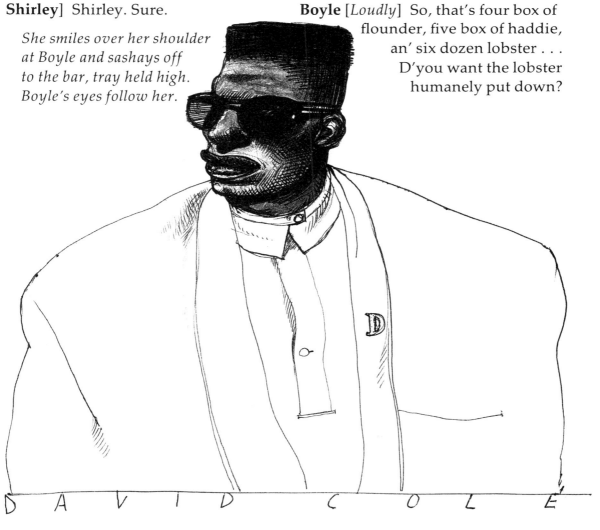

D A V I D   C O L E

Shirley [*To the barman*] Pour us a Longlife, Spencer.

She glances over her shoulder at the corner banquette.

Shirley [*To Tracey*] Told you he was a doll, didn't I?

Tracey] Yeh, the kind you'd like to stick pins into.

Back at the abandoned factory site Frank is leaning against the passenger door of the taxi wolfing down the remainder of his Clambake leftovers.
    The taxi's bonnet is up, and Billie is underneath it.

Frank] You sure you don't want to try some? Friend of mine in Aberfoyle flies a planeload of this scoff across to Maxim's twice a week.

Billie [*Under bonnet*] Thanks, I'll bear that in mind next time I phone up for a res . . . ha! It's just fell into place!

Frank] Good, you can drive us back to the *Echo*, I've got a feelin' I might've . . .

Billie [*Emerging*] 'Crabmeat Crepes A Feast of Fun for Fifties Freaks at Faifley's "Pancake Roadhouse"', right?

Frank] Eh?

Billie] I thought I recognised the kisser, I just couldnae put a quote to it.

Frank] God, fancy you rememberin' that.

Billie] How could I ever forget?

Frank] You and my Features Editor.

Billie] That's where Dorwood took us for my birthday . . . talk about bum steers?

She reaches in to the taxi and unhooks the mike.

Frank] Who's Dorwood?

He stuffs more seafood into his mouth.

Billie] Typical . . . doesnae even read his own newspaper.
[*On radio*] Car Fourteen to base, over?
[*To Frank*] Dorwood Crouch and the Deadwood Playboys, they're a Country an' Western outfit.

Frank] Away.

Billie] Correction . . . used to be a Country an' Western outfit.
[*On radio*] You there, Jolene?

Frank] Ah . . . crossed over to Motown, have they? A suitably lumpen compromise.

There is a burst of static over the radio

Billie [*On radio*] Yeh, Jolene, you'll find a coupla thumb picks in my coat, gonnae chuck them in your saddle bags for us, over?

After a 'Ten Four' on the radio she hooks the mike up.

Billie] You ever listen to any their albums?

Frank] Thought you were a gonnae ask her to phone up a garage . . . Jolene, naw?

Billie goes back under the bonnet.

Billie] They brung their last one out as a tribute to Johnny Cash . . . played it all through their trial on Radio Clyde . . .

Frank piles more shellfish into his mouth.

Billie] Dorwood and the Deadwoods . . .

She pops her head out.

Billie] *Live at the Bar-L.*

Frank gags on his seafood cocktail.

Billie] S'up with you?

Frank] Bugger me, that's it!

Billie] Ironic? Yeh, that's what I said to Jolene.

She bangs the bonnet shut.

Cissie is cautiously checking the banquettes at the Bar-L for any sign of Fraser Boyle.
    Frank enters from the street.

Frank [*Over shoulder*] Chuck moanin', you'll get your dough!

Billie trails in his wake.

Frank [*Surprised*]
    Hey, it is quite snazzy.

He casts his eyes around the interior.

Billie] Nineteen fifty, right!
Frank] Bevis Hillier you ain't, Shorty. That plasterwork is almost certainly art deco . . .

He looks at Billie.

Frank] . . . awright, awright, ersatz deco but it's still a lot earlier than . . .
Billie [*Interrupting*] Your taxi fare, it's nineteen pounds fifty.

Shirley approaches them, a big smile at the ready.

Shirley [*To Frank*] Hi, can I find you a stool?
Frank] Naw, I'll just kill her with my bare hands . . .
Shirley] I'm sorry?
Frank] It's her that should be apologisin' . . . twenty quid for a world tour of the City Centre?

Billie leans forward.

Billie] You couldnae cash this balloon a cheque, could you?
Shirley] Pardon me?
Frank] Not to mention the Hank Williams tapes an' a short wave bandit called Jolene . . .

He shrugs off his Burberry.

Frank] I'll perch up at the Steinway, if you don't mind, sweetheart.

He piles his coat into Shirley's arms.

Shirley] It's a Blüthner. [*Loudly*] Tracey?
Billie] Look, if I don't get my dough I'm phonin' the polis.

Frank catches sight of Cissie making her way back to the kitchen.

Frank [*Smitten*] Yeah, you do that . . .

Tracey strolls up.

Shirley [*In passing*] Stick this jerk at the pianna, will you?
Billie] Ho, I'm talkin' to you.
Tracey [*To Frank*] Hi, are you together?
Frank] What you talkin' about, I'm always together . . .

He spills his cigarettes on to the floor as he tags along behind Tracey who leads the way to the piano.

Frank [*Over his shoulder to Billie*] Sixties' patter's obviously back in.

But Billie is no longer there.
  Cissie exits from the kitchen, and Frank tries catching her eye.

Frank] Right on, yeah?

He walks straight into the piano.

Frank [*Softly*] Ohyah.
Tracey] Can I get you a drink?

Frank glances in Cissie's direction.

26

Frank] Yeah . . . bring us somethin' long an' cool, will you?

Tracey] Tonight's Specials are Lobster Creole in a Blue Cheese Dip and Crawdaddy Claws with a side order of Clam Chowder . . .

Frank pales at the very mention.

Tracey] Sorry, what was your bar order again?

Billie's head appears above the piano lid.

Billie] Big glass of ginger, plenty ice.

Frank] I thought you were away phonin' the . . . bwoop!

His hand flies to his mouth.

Billie] You shut your face or I'll tell them who you are.

Tracey] How . . . who is he?

Frank] 'Scuse me . . . bwoop.

He slides off the piano stool, and hotfoots it for the men's room.

Billie] Did I ask for ice? I cannae quite . . .

Tracey [*Loudly*] One Seven-Up, out the freezer!

She moves off.
Cissie appears at Billie's other shoulder, order pad at the ready.

Cissie] Hi, would you care to order?

She gives Billie a dazzling smile as

David Cole passes on his way back from the men's room.
Billie glances at her Hopalong Cassidy watch.

Billie] Yeah, I suppose I might have somethin' before Jolene . . .

Cissie slips away as soon as David Cole has gone past.

Billie] . . . gets here.

She looks around for Cissie.

Tracey [*To Shirley*] Night Of A Thousand Stars, did you say? There's another one just hightailed it into the lavvy.

The men's room is deserted.
The painful sound of retching reverberates around the marble-tiled walls.
Just visible in the gap under a cubicle door is a pair of well-worn highly ornate cowboy boots.

Frank [*Echoey*] Aw, God . . .

The boots are joined by a pair of stout brogues in the next cubicle but one. The brogues are attached to a pair of Harris Tweed pegbottoms on their knees.
There is a long moment of silence. Then . . .

Frank [*Echoey, sings*] 'Well, since ma baby left me, I found a new place to dwell . . .'

Frank has his head down the faux-marble toilet bowl, his hand groping for loo paper.

Frank [*Sings*] 'It's down at the end of Lonely Street, call' Heartbreak Hotel . . . doo-doo doo-doo . . . heartbreak is so lonely . . . doo-doo doo-doo . . . heartbreak is so lonely . . . doo-doo doo-doo . . . heartbreak is so lonely, I could . . .'

There is a splintering crash as the cubicle door is booted in.
   Frank lifts his head out of the toilet bowl as Fraser Boyle's gloved fist smashes into his face.

Out in the bar Jolene, splendid in fringed jacket and Stetson hat, has joined Billie by the piano.

Jolene] What d'you mean, what kept me? I'd to put away all my maps an' hose out the drivers' toilets. That's your rodeo boots . . .

She plonks a pair of boots on the piano lid.

Jolene] Car Twenty-Six says you can get Western-style Odor Eaters from the wee cobbler's next door to the bookie's shop in Maryhill Road.

Billie looks suitably embarrassed.

Billie] Thanks, Jolene.

Jolene tugs at the bandana knotted round her throat.

Jolene] God, it's really bilin' in here, d'you think we could ask somebody to open a windae?

David Cole resumes his seat at the piano and launches into a selection from the recent Broadway musicals catalogue.

Billie] Gonnae shuttup, Jolene?
Jolene [*To Cole*] Give us the nod if you're gonnae play any Jim Reeves numbers . . .

She gets a dig from Billie.

Jolene] . . . so we can skedaddle. [*To Billie*] What you pokin' us for? I should've got Car Twenty-Six to get you they insoles . . . did the guy not tell you them frog boots were rubber when you tried them on?

Billie] Aw, God . . .

Billie covers her face with her hands.

Jolene [*To Cole*] You don't happen to know anybody that wants to buy a moped, do you?

Cissie approaches them on her way to the kitchen.

Jolene [*Loudly*] 'Scuse me? [*To Billie*] D'you want a plate of chips?

Billie's head sinks slowly on to the piano lid.

Billie] I'm not with you, Jolene . . .
Jolene] God, look who it is, Billie!

Cissie sails past into the kitchen.

Cissie [*From kitchen*] Five Tamali, one Devildog!
Billie] I'm not with you, I said.
Jolene] It's her that used to sing with the Driftin' Tumbleweeds before they split up.

Billie looks up.

Billie] Where?
Jolene] The big skelf in the car smash hairdo, she just went through that door.
Billie] Och, your bum.
Jolene] Cross ma heart an' hope to die, she just shoved that door open an' went straight through it. D'you not remember the pair of us done a duet with her at the OK Korral in Kilwinning? Dorwood was on the jumbo . . .
Billie] Comin' back from Kentucky?
Jolene] The twelve-string jumbo, quit actin' it . . . you were wearin' this stupit poncho an' she had on these brilliant buckskin chaps . . . d'you remember now?
Billie] Naw, I don't, it's about ten years since we last played the OK, an' it was you that was wearin' the stupit poncho, not me, right!

Meanwhile, in the men's room at the Bar-L Fraser Boyle has removed his gloves and is running his knuckles under the tap.

Frank] You'll never guess who else I bumped into the night.

The loo flushes, and Frank emerges from the cubicle, jacket in hand. His nose is swollen and bloody.

Frank] Gordon Smart.

He crosses to the basins, and chucks his jacket on top of Boyle's fish order book.

Boyle] Wee guy with a humph?
Frank] Naw, that was Wee Humphrey . . .

He turns the taps on.

Boyle] I don't recall any Gordon Smart, sure you got the name right?
Frank] You must . . . he was the only guy in the entire history of St Saviour's that could say the whole of the *De Profundis* without wettin' his trousers . . .

Frank examines his damaged nose in the mirror.

Frank] . . . big yella teeth . . . used to wear a Cecil Gee shurt with a monogram on the pocket.

He gives his face a tentative splash.

Boyle] Cecil Gee? Nup, doesnae get the recollective juices goin'.

He gives his knuckles a suck.

Frank] Lugged his homework books about in a toilet bag with succulents all over it . . .
Boyle] With what all over it?

Frank] . . . succulents. Big fan of Wishbone Ash an' the Beverley Sisters. His Maw was an invalid . . . never away from the chapel.
Boyle] Hold on, hold on . . .
Frank] Snappy dresser.
Boyle] Snappy dresser . . . wore these weird shurts wi' somebody's initials on the pocket?
Frank] You want to see him now.
Boyle] Doin' well, is he?

Boyle moves to the hand-drier.

Boyle] Couldnae draw cowboys, as I remember.
Frank] Cannae draw teeth either. Not long dropped outta dental college, he was tellin' me.

Boyle] S'that what he done? Somebody told me he'd snuffed it. What about yourself, what you been up to?

He stabs on the hand-drier, rendering Frank's résumé of his career totally inaudible, but he carries on anyway.

Frank [*Under hand-drier racket*] Aw, this 'n' that . . . managed to get a job sellin' holy pitchers an' second-hand pullovers offa stall at the Barras when I left St Saviour's, that lasted about a fortnight . . . then I went into surgical hosiery, stuck that for seven months, it was murder . . . what'd I do then? Aw, yeh . . . saw this advert for a Mobile Librarian in the *Dundee Courier* . . . spent the next year an' a half drivin' about Angus in a converted ambulance dolin' out *True Detective* an' cowboy books to the natives . . . thought I was gonnae go off ma head . . . eventually got the heave for chuckin' fourteen hundredweight of Annie S Swans into a skip in Forfar . . . took to ma bed for a year, read a lotta Descartes . . . which is where I got the notion to go to university . . . plan was to read French literature but that would've meant learnin' French so I settled for philosophy an' economics . . .

bought myself a Hofner Senator to replace the one ma old man made into a coffee table . . . started goin' wi' this knockout doll wi' buck teeth an' a Ferrari, managed to clinch a pretty poor 'second', got myself a job on the *Evening Echo*, spearheadin' their telephone advertisin' department . . . shifted us from there on to the Rab Haw column when the incumbent went down wi' dysentery after dinin' out in Faifley . . . been there ever since . . .

As the blower whines to a stop, Boyle recrosses to the mirror to comb his greased-back pompadour.

Frank] . . . how's about you?

He crosses to the roller-towel.

Frank] Last I heard you were studyin' for the priesthood.

Billie is driving the taxi, and Jolene is crammed in the back with the moped, accordion case, guitar, 5-watt amp and togs.

Billie [*Over shoulder*] I promise you, Jolene, I remember distinctly your Mum gettin' the knittin' pattern out of her *Woman's Realm* . . . it had

these big reindeers gallopin' round the hole you put your head through.

Jolene] They werenae reindeer, they were caribou . . . an' it was the *Red Star Weekly*. The *Woman's Realm* never done ponchos . . . tea cosies, yes . . . ponchos, naw.

Billie] You wanted to look like Emmylou Harris, I remember.

Jolene] Aye, well you ought to know, it was you that wore it . . . an' you looked like bloody *Rolf* Harris, so there!

Billie] What was it we sang again . . . you, me, and the beanpole?

Jolene] I thought you couldnae remember?

Billie] I cannae, what d'you suppose I'm askin' for? It wasnae 'Pistol Packin' Mama', was it?

Jolene] Don't be ridiculous.

Billie] 'Tennessee Wig Walk'?

Jolene] Naw!

Billie] What was it, well?

Jolene] See if you ever tell anybody I wore a poncho I'm gonnae batter your melt in, Billie McPhail!

Billie muses momentarily.

Billie] Naw, I'm pretty sure it wasnae a Kristofferson number, Jolene.

★ ★ ★

By now Cissie has started clearing empty glasses from the Bar-L piano top.

Fraser Boyle emerges from the men's room, pulling his gloves on. He spots Cissie, does a double take, then approaches stealthily and places his face close to her ear.

Boyle] Boo.
Cissie] Waaaaah!

She drops the tray with a crash.
David Cole's head appears above the banquette.

Tracey] There she's tryin' to get off with your lumber, Shirley.
Cissie] I might well ask you the same . . . what does it look like I'm doin'? Out my road.

She bends down to clear up the broken glass.

Boyle] Yeh, smart thinkin' . . . best not goin' near all thon dough till the dust settles.
Cissie] All what dough? Lift your feet.
Boyle] You been in to see the boy yet? I dig the hairdo.
Cissie] What boy is this?
Boyle] Naw, you suit it, honest . . . lotsa guys would get put off, not

me. Dorwood . . . up the Bar-L . . . listen, do us a favour, will you? Next time you're in to visit him, tell him Fraser Boyle managed to get him back his Dobro.

Cissie's face comes up level with Boyle's.

Cissie] Dobro?
Boyle] Aye, s'a geetar with resonator pan in the middle . . . the guy he lent it to just lost all his fingers in an unlucky . . .
Cissie [*Interrupting***]** I know what a Dobro is, I'm just wonderin' how come you couldn't've told him about it yourself . . . were you not in court this mornin'? Shift.

She tries to push past, but Boyle blocks her way.

Boyle] Have a heart, sugar, I'm hardly goin' to stand up in the public benches an' go 'Scuse me, Dorwood, sorry to hear you're gettin' locked down for seven years but I've got your Dobro sittin' outside in a brown paper poke' . . . that cruel I'm arenae.
Cissie] Hold on, hold on . . . is this the same Fraser Boyle that stood at the curb an' sang two verses of 'Ole Shep' 'cos next door's alsatian just went under a Dodge City delivery truck, while his eld . . .

Boyle [*Interrupting*] Naw, you've got it all wrong, darlin' . . .

Cissie] . . . while his elderly mother was lyin' in a hosptal bed gettin' penicillin jags for lockjaw?

Boyle] Naw, you've definitely got it . . .

Cissie [*Interrupting again*] I think we can drop the Mr Sensitive act. If you've got anythin' to give to Dorwood, you give it to him, I'm not your dogsbody!

She shoves him aside and heads for the kitchen.

Boyle] Ho, come back here, you've got it all wrong . . .

Cissie disappears into the kitchen, and Shirley crosses to the piano.

Shirley] Hi, can I get you somethin'?

Boyle] Stupit bitch, it was an airedale.

Shirley's smile evaporates.

Shirley] Okay, cool it cowboy, I'm not a mind-reader. [*Loudly*] One Airedale! [*To Boyle*] D'you want a slice of lemon in it?

In the men's room Frank is investigating the damage done to his nose in the mirror.

Frank] Awright, so we all of us revere His Pelvic Majesty's memory but God Almighty . . .

A diner enters and crosses to one of the cubicles.

Frank] He was exactly the same at St Saviour's . . . set fire to six of the Janitor's rabbits when he sluiced all his Elvis pin-ups down the urinals . . . welded the woodwork teacher's goggles to the front bumper of his Lambretta after gettin' three outta fifty for his plywood cutout of 'The King', when we were supposed to be makin' coat pegs outta gash timber for the *Gang Show*.

He picks up his jacket.

Frank] If you're thinkin' about stickin' your napper down the pan an' givin it laldy, don't whatever you do, pick anythin' from the Sun Records catalogue, pre-'57 . . .

He slips his arms into the jacket sleeves.

Frank [*Continues*] . . . he's liable to burst in here an' splatter your brains all over the sanitary-ware.

He picks up Boyle's order book.

Frank] Stupit grizzly's left his Filofax . . .

★ ★ ★

*In the smoky back-room of a
pub, that doubles as the
Cactus Club on alternative
evenings, Billie and Jolene
are onstage singing.*

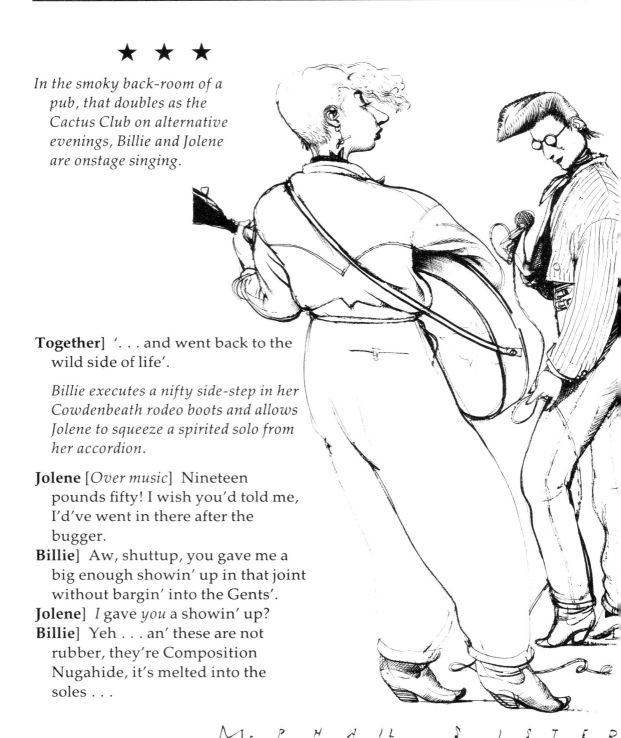

Together] '. . . and went back to the
wild side of life'.

*Billie executes a nifty side-step in her
Cowdenbeath rodeo boots and allows
Jolene to squeeze a spirited solo from
her accordion.*

Jolene [*Over music*] Nineteen
pounds fifty! I wish you'd told me,
I'd've went in there after the
bugger.
Billie] Aw, shuttup, you gave me a
big enough showin' up in that joint
without bargin' into the Gents'.
Jolene] *I* gave *you* a showin' up?
Billie] Yeh . . . an' these are not
rubber, they're Composition
Nugahide, it's melted into the
soles . . .

M c P H A I L   S I S T E R

She holds up a boot for inspection and then leans into the mike.

Billie [*Sings*] 'If I had the wings of an angel . . .'

Back at the Bar-L Cissie is leaning up against the back of an unoccupied banquette reading Tracey's Echo. *Frank sneaks up behind her and peeks over her shoulder.*

Frank] Aw, well done.

Cissie [*Surprised*] I wish people wouldn't keep doin' that! What d'you want?

Frank] I thought one of the other dolls was goin' to beat you to it.

Frank plucks a pen from Cissie's pocket and starts scribbling on a small card from his coat pocket.

Frank] Who's the lucky guy?

Cissie] You're not talkin' to me, are you?

Frank] If you take my advice, you'll give the Pancake Roadhouse in Faifley the go-by . . .

He hands the card to Cissie.

Cissie] What's this? [*Reading*] 'Bon appetit. That fabulous "Dinner for Two" is yours. Signed Rab Haw'.

Frank's signature and phone number are scrawled along the bottom of the card.

Frank] Any problems just ring that number . . . there's one or two of the eateries listed overleaf that aren't fully conversant with the scheme as yet but we're hopin' to . . .

Cissie [*Interrupting*] I don't know what it is you're sellin' but it's no sale. Sorry.

She stuffs the card back into Frank's top pocket.

Frank] Naw, naw. I know when I've been rumbled. Here . . .

He takes the card from his pocket and hands it to Cissie.

Cissie] Too right you have.

She rams the card back into Frank's top pocket.

Frank] Okay, so you didn't go through the ritual of rappin' me on the raincoat with your rolled-up copy of the *Echo*, an recitin' the rubric 'You are Rab Haw and I claim my intimate candlelit dinner for two', but rules are there to be bent. Please . . .

Cissie takes the thrice-proffered card.

Frank] That entitles you and your partner to the free sparkling red of your choice . . .

Cissie rips the card in two . . .

Frank] . . . plus a second cup of coffee . . .

. . . and rips the two pieces into four . . .

Frank] . . . and the Black Forest gateau.

Cissie tears the four pieces into eight . . .

Frank] If they've got any.

Cissie lets the torn pieces of card flutter to the floor.

Frank] You didn't happen to notice where the hardnut in the high heels went, did you?

He tries nonchalantly glancing round the room and fails.

Cissie] You'll be a friend of his, yeah?

Frank] Depends what you mean by a friend . . . we don't exchange Christmas cards or nothin'.

He holds out Boyle's order book.

Frank] He left his . . .

Cissie [*Interrupting*] Quick, order somethin'.

She shoves Frank into the banquette and whips out her pad.

Frank] Eh?

Cissie] . . . and would that be with the Clam Chowder or without the Clam Chowder?

She gives Frank a big smile as David Cole 'circulates' in their direction.

Frank] Er . . . without, I think. This's a wind-up, right?

David Cole] Hey . . . the footwear, man.

He regards Frank's brogues with wry amusement.

Frank] Aw, naw, don't tell me . . .

Frank bends down to inspect the soles of his shoes to discover what he's stood in.

David Cole] Outtasight, baby . . . outtasight.

He moves off, chuckling.

Frank] What is this, Sixties Patter Fortnight?

Cissie] S'that what they call you in these parts, yeah?

Frank] What?

Cissie] The Footwear Man?

Frank snatches pen from Cissie.

Frank [*Writing*] . . . cheeky waitresses.

He folds his 'Reporter's Shorthand Notepad' shut and hands the pen back to Cissie.

Cissie] Come off it, you can buy they notebooks in Woolie's.

Frank] Yeh, you tell that to the big guy in the white tux when he opens the morra night's edition an' there it is starin' him in the kisser . . . 'Bolshie Broads and Bum Service Bug Our Man at Bar-L' . . . give us that pen back, I forgot to take down your number.

Cissie] Don't act it, you're not a reporter.

Frank] I'm an investigative journalist, you're just after droolin' over my picture in the *Echo*.

Cissie] Your tonsils. Where?

She unfurls the newspaper and starts riffling through it.

Frank] Don't *you* act it . . .

He snatches the paper.

Frank] . . . there I am there in the mid . . . hey, there's Dorwood . . .

Cissie] Gimme that.

She attempts to snatch the paper back.

Frank] It's one of those days, innit? You ever read Koestler's *The Roots of* . . .

Cissie manages to grab the paper.

Cissie] What the bloody hell has Koestler got to do with Dorwood gettin' sent to jail for seven years!

Frank] Seven years? What'd he do, a cover version of 'Tiny Bubbles'?

Tracey has noticed Cissie laying into Frank with the shredded Evening Echo *and goes over to the manager.*

Tracey] I don't like to bother you, Mr Cole, but I've got a feeling one of the diners might like a word.

She jerks a thumb over her shoulder.

As the sickle moon melts into a slithering serpent on the rippling waters of the river Clyde, Frank, leaning on a parapet, flicks idly through Fraser Boyle's forgotten order book.

Frank] I remember once when I was about ten I had to wait seven weeks for a letter to arrive from my pen-pal in the States . . .

He fingers a brown envelope he has found between the pages of the order book.

Frank] . . . thought I was goin' to die before it got here.

He holds the envelope up to the light.

Frank] Seven years . . .?

Cissie sits hunched up on a bench, Frank's outsize Burberry belted tightly around her.
She leans an arm on the benchback, one hand held to her forehead.

Frank] . . . I'm not sure I could wait that long for anythin'.

Cissie] If that's an invitation, the answer's 'Get lost, buster.'

Frank] Naw, I didn't mean it like that, I meant . . .

Cissie looks at him.

Frank] . . . I didnae, honest. I'm not that kinda guy.

Cissie] You're all that kinda guy.

She stands up.

Frank] You don't believe in makin' it easy, do you? I'm tryin' my best to be sympathetic here.

Cissie] Well, don't bother, it's nauseatin'.

Cissie takes off across the bridge nearby.

Frank [*Getting up*] Look, I realise you must be upset at losin' your ball'n'chain but it wasn't entirely my . . .

38

He takes off after her.

Cissie] If that's meant to be an apology it's only just this side of adequate . . . try rephrasin' it.

Frank] An apology! Listen, ya lanky big get . . .

He catches up with Cissie and grabs her sleeve.

Cissie] Uh uh . . . Start again.

Frank] Who was it was batterin' lumps outta who back there, hmmmm?

Cissie] Think yourself lucky, if you'd been a man I'd've socked you in the teeth . . . an' just in case you got the wrong end of the stick from that rotten rag you work for, Dorwood didn't do any of that stuff they said he did . . . he might be a header but he's hardly into snortin' coke an' holdin' anybody up with a hammer.

Frank] How can you be so . . .

Cissie [*Interrupting*] Because I know Dorwood, don't I?

She sets off again.

Frank [*To himself*] Yeh, an' so does at least one Patsy Cline-clone of my acquaintance . . .

He starts walking after Cissie.

Cissie] God almighy, it's all I can do to get him to hold up a shelf while I put the nails in, he's that feeble! As for drugs . . .

Frank] How's about Dwane, mebbe it was him that put Dorwood up to . . .

Cissie [*Interrupting again*] Dwane's just a dumplin'. If you want to know who the real culprit is . . . och, what's the point, you're like all the rest . . . why don't you just beat it?

She stops and looks at Frank.

Frank] Eh?

Cissie] You heard . . . blow . . . vamoose.

She pulls Frank's Burberry round her and strides angrily off.

Frank] How can I vamoose? This's my night for gettin' the grease stains out of my Burberry, dammit!

Outside the Cactus Club Billie and Jolene are loading their gear into the taxi.

Billie] Wonder how Dorwood's gettin' on, eh?

Jolene] At least he'll be gettin' somethin' to eat where he is . . .

Billie] You know perfectly well we've got to make up the shortfall in wur taxi float, which is still

seven bucks short, by the way . . .
I'm gonnae have to stop off at my
mother's an' ask for a bung . . .
'time is it?

Jolene] Ten past twelve, God, I could
happily bite the reindeers offa
poncho, she'll not still be up, will
she?

Billie] Who willnae?

Jolene] Your Maw.

*They climb into the taxi, Billie in the
front and Jolene in the back.*

Billie] Jolene, my 'Maw' died on the
fourteenth of March, you wore
thon shurt with the tommyhawks
on it to her funeral . . .

Jolene] Aw, yeh, so I did . . .

Billie] . . . a bung off our Raymond
I'm talkin' . . . [*She starts the
engine*] He's strippin' the
wallpaper in the lobby.

Jolene] What's he doin' that for?

Billie] My Mammy always hated it.

Jolene] That's what I mean, what's
he doin' it now for?

Billie] 'Cos he's got his work to go to
durin' the day . . . honest to God,
see you, you can be right obtuse at
times, Jolene.

She revs the taxi engine.

*On a street corner near the river Frank
and Cissie are still arguing.*

Frank] You take that off again and
you're getting smacked, right!

*He pulls the Burberry tight around
Cissie.*

Cissie] Right!

Frank] Right!
He lets go.

Cissie] I'll post it on to you, right!

Frank] Right!

They walk on.

Cissie] You don't know what it's like
goin' back to an empty flat an' his
Wranglers are all shrivelled up over
the radiators an' the phone never
goes an' the clingfilm's come off his
Randy Travis records an' lies about
the carpet like ectoplasm an' the
neighbours stuff things through
your letterbox an' write these foul
letters an' you cannae get anythin'
from the grocer's without payin'
cash an' . . .

Frank stops.

Frank] You'll post what on to me?

Cissie] This coat.

Frank] Talk sense, by the time you
get it into a Jiffy Bag you'll not have
enough spittle left to lick the . . .
don't you dare take that off again,
I'm warnin' you!

He grabs Cissie by the lapels.

Cissie] Aaaaarg, ma chest!

Back at his flat, Frank is standing in the middle of a chaotic kitchenette, a piece of charred toast on the worktop in front of him.

Frank [*Shouts*] D'you want me to spread some butter on it? Or mebbe you'd prefer some . . .

He takes a grimy container down from the shelf.

Frank] . . . treacle?

He unscrews the top of the container and sniffs the contents.

In the adjoining room, Cissie, in a pair of Frank's pyjamas, is perusing a pinboard. It is covered in newspaper clippings and snapshots (including one of a youthful Frank with big guitar and Elvis leer), restaurant invites, yellowing book reviews, Doris Day cutouts, unpaid bills, publishers' rejection slips, et al.

Cissie's attention is caught by a clipping from the Glasgow Herald *dated 1976. It shows a line of mug shots with a headline above that reads*

'Kelvinside Four jailed for incitement'. *The 'K 4' (two male and two female) are: Henderson (M), Brolly (F), Melon (F), and McClusky (a younger Frank).*

The sub-heading under the photographs reads: '90 days apiece for pot-smoking "Maoists" '.

Frank wobbles through from the kitchen with a tray.

Frank] Wire in.

He places the tray with non-matching crockery on a low table.

The studio apartment, a converted loft in a one-time cheese factory, is a large airy room with bare floorboards, a mattress, a battered typewriter, a broken (but still working) telephone, a 50s' wireless set, a 30s' armchair, and 'enormous potential'.

It is also unbelievably untidy.

Cissie] You not havin' any?
Frank] I ate awready.

Cissie bites into the toast and freezes.

Frank] Marmite. 'Many sugars?
Cissie] I don't . . . thanks.

She picks up a mug and crosses to the window.

Cissie] 'Long've you lived in this dump?
Frank] Aw, about six . . . what d'you mean, this dump? I'll have you

know this property's listed in at least one agent's books as a 'des con enviably adj to "Merchant City"' . . .

Cissie looks out of the window at a clutch of winos huddled around burning garbage on the wasteground opposite.

Cissie] Yeh, an' these'll be some of the 'merchants' havin' themselves an informal Round Table tête-à-tête over a glass of Buckfast 'Nouveau', I presume?

Frank] Where?

He joins Cissie at the window.

Cissie] I've just twigged . . .

- C I S S I E -

42

She turns away from the window and wanders back across the room.

Frank] Twigged what?

Cissie] . . . how come, after claimin' to be an investigative journalist, you were at some pains to point out the difference between your 'part-time food an' wine correspondent with shoogly shorthand and an overdraft that would choke a Clydesdale' and your 'hard-nosed crime reporter with one foot in the underworld an' . . .'

Frank [*Interrupting*] Aw, God, we're not harpin' back to that again.

Cissie] Naw, naw, I don't blame you . . . I mean, ex-junkie jailbirds with extreme political views cannae be too careful when it comes to . . .

Frank [*Indignantly*] 'Ex-junkie jailbirds' nothin'! It was the two dames that rolled this big joint an' got me an' that other mug at the end there to pap eggs at the Home Secretary . . .

He peers at the pinboard.

Frank] . . . it was the Home Secretary, wasn't it? Anyway, some balloon that arrived on campus to deliver a two-hour diarretic on 'inner city unrest' an' to raffle a set of water-skis on behalf of the Toryglen Young Conservatives.

Cissie] It says here you were 'Maoists'.

Frank] That's only 'cos we ran outta ammunition an' my compadre, Henderson, high on moral outrage an' a hefty dose of marijuana, flang what was left of his carry-out Chinky at the Rector . . . look, we know that Fraser Boyle wasn't in the motor the night Dorwood got arrested for the simple reason that he stayed behind at the what-d'-you-me-cry-it . . .

Cissie] OK Korral.

Frank] . . . to pack up their banjos 'n' stuff, it said it in the paper.

Cissie] An' you believe everythin' you read in the paper, right?

Frank] Not all of it, naw . . . the trouble with you is you just cannae face up to the fact that you married a nutter.

Cissie] An' the trouble with you is you just don't listen . . . I'm the first to admit he's a nutter. I mean, who in their right senses jacks in a deep-sea divin' career to become a Deadwood Playboy?

Frank] Deep-sea divin'?

Cissie] That's what he got into after The Driftin' Tumbleweeds broke up . . . things were fine till he bumped into Fraser Boyle in a submersible just south of Piper Omega an' started swappin'

Country albums with a trouble-shooter called Dwane . . . we all know what happened then. What sticks in my craw is that Fraser Boyle's still at liberty to drive about in his fish motor dispensin' threats an' menaces along with the lemon sole an' God-only-knows-what-else, while dopey Dorwood keeps his gub shut an' carries the can for the next seven years!

Frank] Lemme get this right . . . are you sayin' it was Boyle that tipped off . . .

Cissie] Who else would it be! He was eaten up with envy right from the off . . . whatever Dorwood had, Boyle wasnae happy till he'd wasted it . . . the big Everly Brothers picture he had in the bathroom, Boyle blacked their teeth out . . . the Hank Williams souvenir toaster he got from the States, Boyle put Kraft cheese slices in it . . . the Slim Whitman autographed doyley his Auntie Kathleen got at the Empire in 1955, Boyle made it into a parachute . . . he's a jealous bastard, the guy.

Frank] An' not just jealous . . . I've seen him puttin' squibs in a school chum's blazer an' tyin' his wrists to the fire extinguisher . . . d'you want to see the scorch marks?

Cissie] So you'll help me nail him, yeh?

Frank stuffs his shirt back into his trousers.

Frank] I wish I could but I can't . . . I just cannae . . . you want to see the workload I've got . . . two screenplays, four hardback reviews, one of them for the *TLS* . . . not to mention an overdue anthology of Georgian poetry and a probing piece on Potato Puffs for the Christmas issue of the *Grocer* . . .

There is a knocking at the front door.

Frank] . . . Who the hell can that be at this time of night?

He crosses to the hallway.

Frank [*To Cissie*] Help yourself to more coffee.

Cissie] Yeh . . . thanks.

Frank exits to the hallway. There is more knocking.

Frank] That's right, chap the door down!

Cissie crosses to the kitchen and surveys the mess of burnt pots, manky dishes, the remains of a thousand frozen dinners, overflowing buckets, filthy cooker . . . and is appalled.

Cissie] God, what a cowp.

She hears voices from the hall.

Frank] Aw, naw, I thought I'd got
shot of you . . .
Jolene] Okay pal, taxi money, stump
up.
Frank] Ohyah!

*On a parapet by the riverside the pages
of Boyle's order book flutter in the
breeze. A filthy mit with horny nails
closes over the book and picks it up.
    A derelict with a toilet bag covered
all over in succulents, leafs through
the book, removes the carbon paper
and blows his nose on it. As he is
about to drop the order book into a
litter bin a brown envelope falls out
on to the pavement.
    The derelict drops the book into the
bin and bends to retrieve the
envelope. He peels back a corner flap,
lifts it to his nose and sniffs.*

*In the Bar-L a selection of jazz-tinged
Smokey Robinson hits underpins the
hum of conversation from the late-
night diners.*

*There is a faint screech of brakes
from outside, followed by the
slamming of a van door.
    Fraser Boyle shoulders his way in
from the street, knocking Tracey aside
in his headlong dash for the men's
room.*

Tracey] That's your cowpokes for
you, Shirley . . . cannae hold their
Airedales.

*Cissie has finally located the coffee pot
under some debris in Frank's kitchen
and is pouring some into a mug when
Frank appears in the doorway.*

Frank] Er . . . I hate to ask, but I don't
suppose you could see your way to
lendin' me nineteen pounds fifty,
could you?

Billie [*Shouting from the hall*] Naw,
Jolene . . . don't!

*There is splintering crash from the
hall.*

*There is another splintering crash as
Fraser Boyle boots in the cubicle doors
in the Bar-L men's room.*

Fraser
Boyle

2

The Eagle of the Apocalypse and the Sidewinders of Satan

SATURDAY / SUNDAY

There is a Turneresque sunrise over the river Clyde.

Through the mist a River Police launch can be seen. A tattered topcoat is being dragged from the water.

As the ragged coat is hoisted aboard, a toilet bag covered all over in succulents bobs to the surface. A brown envelope floats in the middle of the powdery scum that forms on the undulating waters.

Frank McLusky is scrubbing his teeth in front of the bathroom mirror.

There is the sound of a hoover from the other room, and he hears a muffled voice shouting at him.

Frank [*Loudly*] What'd you say?

He turns his head. His face contorts in agony.

Frank] Aaaaahyah . . .

Frank, in boxer shorts, woolly vest, and thick socks, clutches at his lower back with one hand while gripping the basin with the other . . . his toothbrush jammed in his mouth.

Cissie Crouch appears at the bathroom door clutching the hoover. She is wearing Frank's Burberry over Frank's pyjamas.

Cissie [*Over noise*] I meant to ask you last night but you looked that cosy tucked up in your armchair I didn't like to waken you.

Frank [*Unintelligibly*] How very thoughtful!

Cissie] Hang on . . .

She disappears.

Frank [*Unintelligibly*] Jesus God . . .

The hoover noise dies down, and Cissie reappears in the doorway.

Cissie] Naw, I thought mebbe with you workin' at the *Echo* you might have one or two contacts on the Country scene, that was all.

Frank [*Unintelligibly*] Yeh, I'm quite pally with the guy that . . .

He reaches up and extracts the toothbrush from his mouth with some difficulty.

Frank] I'm quite pally with the guy that does the 'Farming Outlook' column on a Wednesday . . .

He bends stiffly and splashes water on to his face.

Frank] . . . cycles up from Maybole with his copy in a sheepskin briefcase . . . chuck us that towel, will you?

Cissie's face clouds over.

Cissie] The Country *music* scene.

She chucks a towel at his head.

Frank] Ah, it's a 'scene', is it? I've always regarded it as a 'disaster area', myself . . .

He squeezes past Cissie, drying his face on the towel.
  The apartment has been tidied up beyond recognition.

Frank] What you askin' for?
Cissie] Because it's a good ten years since I set foot in . . .

Frank takes the towel from his face and looks around the room.

Frank [*Interrupting*] Hey, you've hung up my togs.

Frank's 'wardrobe' has been salvaged from the decks and hung neatly on a row of hangers.

Cissie] Yeh, that's gonnae be a slight problem . . .
Frank] I thought I'd lost that . . .

He points to one of the shirts.

Cissie] . . . you're gonnae look a right haddie goin' round the clubs in any them get-ups . . .
Frank] . . . an' there's my corduroys! I was positive they'd walked.
Cissie] . . . people are just goin' to clam up.

Frank pales.

Frank] Please . . . don't say stuff like that.

He slips his arms into the sleeves of his newly found shirt.

Cissie] Well, they are . . . we'll have to think about gettin' you some different . . .
Frank [*Interrupting*] Naw, I meant, please don't mention clams.
Cissie] Are you goin' to listen to me?
Frank] I'm listenin' . . . I'm listenin'.

He wanders across the room.

Cissie] You an' Dorwood're about

the same build, right?

Frank pops his head into the kitchen.

Frank] *And* you've done the kitchen . . .

Frank goes into the now-sparkling kitchen.

Frank] . . . good God, you managed to get the grease off the dishes. I've just been chuckin' them in the bin.

Cissie appears at the doorway behind him.

Cissie] Did you mean what you said last night?

Frank] What . . . 'This armchair's givin' us gyp, I wish that doll in the bed would invite me over to share my own mattress'?

He starts filling the kettle.

Frank] 'Course I meant it . . . ooooow . . .

He puts his hand to his lower back.

Cissie] About doin' somethin' to help Dorwood . . . gimme that.

She takes the kettle and plugs it in.

Frank] Aw, yeh . . . Dorwood . . . I'd forgotten all about him . . .

Frank inches his way out of the kitchen, clutching on to the doorframe.

Frank] . . . I was rather hopin' that you had as well . . . ohyah . . .

Cissie [*From the kitchen*] Yeh, I'll bet you were.

Frank] I mean, it's hardly as if I know the guy . . . you either, come to that. An' I didn't say I'd help him, I said, I'd try an' think of somebody that might.

He crosses the room laboriously to where his corduroy pegbottoms are.

Frank] You thought about goin' to a detective agency? There's one at Anniesland Cross that takes Embassy coupons . . .

Cissie appears at the kitchen door.

Frank] . . . or you could have a word with the Polis . . . tell them it's all been a ghastly mistake, I'm quite sure you'll get a sympathetic . . .

Cissie [*Interrupting*] Will you stop soundin' off for a second an' listen!

Frank freezes, his back to Cissie, bent double with his trousers halfway up his legs.

Frank] Watch it, Ginger . . . just because I let you red up my kitchen, rearrange my wardrobe, an' lend me nineteen pounds fifty for a taxi, that does not give you licence to . . .

Cissie [*Firmly*] Shut up. And you needn't bother haulin' up those trousers, they're only comin' straight back off again.

Frank] I'm sorry, I didn't quite catch . . .

Cissie] You heard . . . get them off.

Frank makes to turn round.

Cissie] Stay where you are, I'm just about to step out of these pyjamas of yours.

Frank] Good God, she's serious . . . [*Aloud*] What made you . . .

His voice cracks. He clears his throat.

Frank] What made you change your mind? You must be nuts about this Dorwood to plump for such a ploy . . . or was it catchin' sight of a manly calf that . . .

Cissie [*Interrupting*] Don't look, I said!

Frank] You'll understand, of course, that I'm possibly not at my best first thing in the mornin' . . . what guy is? 'Specially not after spendin' the night curled up like a kirby grip in my unfavourite armchair . . .

He hobbles across to the mattress, clutching on to his trousers, still bent over.

Frank] . . . but I think I can promise you a forenoon of unparalleled ec . . .

He bends further to slip his trousers off.

Frank [*Softly*] . . . ahyah.

Cissie tucks a borrowed shirt into the waistband of some borrowed trousers.

Cissie] What size are you?

Frank [*Still bent over wrestling with his trousers*] I beg your pardon?

Cissie] Size . . . how big?

Frank] Big? What d'you mean, 'big'?

Cissie] Dorwood's a ten and a half.

Frank [*To himself*] Ten and a half? Good grief . . .

Cissie] You'll be about the same, I fancy . . .

She rolls up her trouser legs and slips her feet into her shoes.

Frank [*Quietly*] Centimetres, we talkin' about, yeh?

Still bent double, Frank measures out 10½ cm with his hands.

Frank] I think you'll find that most medical men . . .

He starts to shuffle painfully across to the mattress again.

Frank] . . . or indeed, most medical women, come to that'll tell you that size is totally irrelevant . . . in fact, I have it on good authority . . .

Cissie [*Interrupting*] Not when it comes to cowboy boots, it isnae.

She looks around for her bag.

Cissie] You don't want to be scliffin' your feet in them.
Frank] Scliffin' my what?
Cissie] Or mebbe you do, you're such an oddball.

She regards the seat of Frank's boxer shorts with a raised eyebrow.

Frank] You ready yet?
Cissie] I'll not be long.
Frank [*Quickly*] Naw, take your time . . . no rush. Hey, we never did settle on what I should call you . . . '4–8–4', perhaps? Mrs Crouch sounds a bit stiff in the circum . . .

He hears the front door slam.

Frank] . . . stances . . . hullo?

He manages to twist round and look with considerable effort.
The room is now empty.

Frank] Well, that's her missed a treat.

He straightens his back, and slowly hauls up his corduroys.

Frank] . . . aaaaaaaaaaaaaaaargh.

Tracey is standing at the counter in the Bar-L, a white 40s' style plug-in telephone to her ear.

Tracey [*On phone*] Yeh, hang on . . .

She holds the receiver against her chest.

Tracey] Give him a shout, Shirley.
Shirley [*Shouts*] Telephone, Mr Cole.
Tracey [*On phone*] If it's a banquette you're after we're fully . . . aw . . .
Shirley] What we supposed to do with this?

She holds up Cissie's 'convict' suit.

David Cole [*To Tracey*] Who is it?
Tracey] The toilet wrecker . . .
David Cole] Huh?

He takes the receiver from Tracey who returns to her sweeping up.

David Cole [*On phone*] Yeh, David Cole, who is this?

Tracey bends down and retrieves the torn fragments of a 'dinner for two' invitation card from the floor.

Shirley] It's never gonnae fit anybody . . .
David Cole [*Still on phone, voice rising*] . . . that's your responsibility, man, I ain't got no more!
Shirley] . . . not even if he puts an advert in the *Echo* for a stiltwalker. Check the gams . . .

She holds the trouser legs against her own.

David Cole [*On phone*] . . . Awright, awright, relax . . . relax . . . lemme find out, huh?

He looks around for Tracey, who is busy piecing together the invitation card with Frank's signature and phone number on it.

David Cole [*To Tracey*] The weirdo in the wing-tip footwear, honey?

Tracey [*To Shirley*] You don't fancy a pancake tea in Faifley, do you?

Cissie has now returned to Frank's apartment and is standing in the doorway draped in several cowboy shirts with a pair of jeans over her arm. She has changed into her own clothes.

Frank is standing in the middle of the room looking down at the very new cowboy boots on his feet.

Cissie] Try strollin' up an' down for a bit.

Frank] Backwards an' forwards, d'you mean?

Frank takes a few tentative steps in his unfamiliar footwear.

Frank] Ohyah . . .

Cissie] Don't point your toes out, it makes you look a right jessie.

Frank] Nup, they're killin' us . . .

He cockles over and starts limping.

Cissie] Keep goin', they just need breakin' in . . . Dorwood never even got to wear them.

Frank] Lucky Dorwood. What they made out of . . . teak?

Cissie] What shirt d'you want?

Frank] I don't want a shirt, I've got a shirt.

Cissie] Here . . . try on these Wranglers.

She loops the jeans over his shoulder.

Frank] S'that where you wear them, yeh?

Cissie] Stop actin' the goat.

Frank reaches out and leans against the wall.

Frank] Would it look stupit if I wore my slippers to the OK Korral? I'm pretty sure the Kilwinning Chapter of the 'Kid-on Cowpokes' wouldnae object to a tenderfoot turnin' up in his baffies . . . you could stitch some fringes round the toecaps, give them a sort of devil-me-care Western look, naw?

Cissie] Are you gonnae take this seriously or . . .

Frank [*Interrupting*] Aw, c'mon, Cissie, you're jokin'. What the hell'm I gonnae discover that the whole of the Strathclyde CID . . . okay, okay, I'm walkin' . . . look, I'm walkin'.

He strides to and fro, his arms swinging.

Frank] How's that?
Cissie] You're not meant to *walk*, you're meant to . . .

She buries her face in the cowboy shirts she's holding.

Cissie [*Muffled*] . . . aaaaaaargh!
Frank] Meant to what . . . mosey, you mean? Lemme try some moseyin' for you . . . watch.

He starts moseyin' around the room.

Frank] You're not watchin', Cissie.
Cissie [*Looking up*] Forget it, awright! It was a stupit idea in the first place . . . gimme those off.
Frank] Naw, naw . . . I just need a bit of practice . . . right, who's this?

He does his John Wayne walk for her.

Frank] He was in *Fort Apache* and *Space Dudes Eat My Ka-Ka* . . . d'you give in?

FRANK

The telephone at his feet rings. Frank bends his knees and picks up the receiver.

Frank [*On phone*] Big Bill Campbell . . . Naw, don't hang up, it's me, Tamara . . . hi. [*To Cissie*] One of my colleagues on the *Echo* . . . [*On phone*] What can I do for you, sweetheart?

Cissie [*Interrupting*] You can post that stuff on to us, okay?

She stuffs the shirts into her bag.

Frank [*To Cissie*] Naw, wait, this might be the very person we're lookin' for . . .

Cissie crosses to the door.

Frank [*To phone*] Can I call you right back, Tama . . . what? Yeh, yeh, right . . . hang on till I get a pencil . . .

He lays the receiver aside.

Frank [*To Cissie*] Silly bugger's on a carphone . . . you're not away, are you? This dame works on the Crime Desk . . .

He hunts around for something to write with.

Frank] It was her that wrote up that stuff on Dorwood's trial. God, see when you tidy up, it's chaos . . .

He hears the sound of the front door slamming again.

Frank] . . . Cissie?

He starts limping across to the door, only to be brought up short by Tamara's small but insistent voice from the phone.
    He doubles back and picks up the receiver.

Frank [*On phone*] Listen, Tamara, I want you to do me a big favour, d'you remember the coupla cowboys that just got . . . what?

Fraser Boyle is in a telephone box in Candleriggs. He's holding a 'Dinner for Two' card, sellotaped together, with Frank McClusky's phone number on it.
    He listens to the engaged signal, and slams the receiver down. He picks it up again and dials Directory Enquiries.

Boyle] C'mon, ya imbecile! [*To phone*] Yeh, City Centre area . . . name of McClusky . . . naw, k-y, like in Jelly . . . F for Francis . . . naw, I've got the number, I just need an address to go with it . . . gonnae hurry up, it's a matter of life an' death!

Frank is still on the phone to Tamara.

Frank [*On phone*] Holy God . . . poor old Gordon, that's tragic . . . I'm really choked . . . naw, I am . . . I happened to bump into him last night quite by . . . wait a minute, the guy was a hobo, what you phonin' me for? I hadnae clapped eyes on him since . . . what!

Frank stands up alarmed.

Frank] Fingerprints . . . what d'you mean, fing . . . what envelope! All I gave the durty dropout was a 'Dinner for Two' card an' a coupla qu . . . aw, God, it's just occurred to me . . . where'd you say they found his . . . naw, skip it, how the hell should I know how the sod got his manky mitts on a . . .

He's interrupted by a loud banging at the front door.

Frank] . . . listen, I'll have to go, Tamara, there's somebody at the . . . Christ, the Polis . . .

There is more loud banging.

Frank [*On phone*] . . . I hope their computer gets a virus, tell them.

Aw, an' listen . . . tell the Features Editor not to worry, I'll keep in t . . . hullo? Buggeration.

He slams the phone down, grabs his Burberry, and hobbles across to the window in his cowboy boots.
     The banging at the front door continues as Frank throws the window up.
     At the front door Fraser Boyle bends down and flips open the letterbox with his gloved finger.

Boyle [*Loudly*] Kissogram for McClusky . . . open up!

A long moment of silence is shattered by a sickening crash as Boyle barges in through the door.
     Once inside he stops and looks around, his eyes light on a blind flapping in the breeze.

Boyle] Aw, classic . . . empty room, open windae, flappin' drapes . . . bugger's legged it down the fire escape.

He clumps across the bare floorboards in his highly-tooled Western footwear.
     Frank cowers in his bathtub behind the half-open bathroom door, and listens.

Boyle] Exceptin', there isnae one.

Boyle's clumping footfalls come to a heart-stopping halt outside the bathroom door.

A rivulet of perspiration trickles the length of Frank's still-swollen nose and falls with a soft plop on to his bunched-up Burberry.

A floorboard creaks.

The half-open bathroom door is pushed full open by an unseen hand. Frank sinks lower in the tub and draws his knees up towards his chin.

A pin might be heard to drop in Dennistoun.

Then . . .

Boyle [*Echoey, sings*] 'Well, since ma baby left me, I've found a new place to dwell . . .'

Boyle, eyes shut, hands braced against the doorframe, has his head thrust inside the echo chamber of the bathroom.

Boyle [*Sings*] ' . . . it's down at the end of Lonely Street, call' Heartbreak Hot . . .'

He breaks off.

Boyle] For God's sake, get a grip, Fraser . . .

He pushes himself backwards off the doorframe and sets about searching the living-room.

Frank, still in the bathtub, twitches spasmodically at each crash and bang as Boyle systematically demolishes the apartment.

The 'studio' is now reduced to an even worse shambles than it was prior to Cissie's tidy-up exercise.

As a final PS, Boyle picks up Frank's treasured Hofner Senator guitar, places an ear to one of the F-holes, and gives it a shake before raising it above his head and bringing it crashing down on to a low table.

Frank stuffs the Burberry into his mouth in an effort to stifle the involuntary squeal of anguish upon hearing the awful splintering 'twang' resonate round and around the bathroom.

A deadly silence ensues.

Then . . .

Boyle [*Quietly sings*] . . . 'Heartbreak is so lonely, baby . . . heartbreak is so lonely . . . doo doo-doo . . . heartbreak is so lonely, I could . . .'

The front door slams.

Slowly, very slowly, Frank straightens his legs and lowers the Burberry from his face.

He stares at the ceiling for several seconds.

Frank] I know you don't exist, but thanks a million . . . ya bastard!

The OK Korral in Kilwinning is a 'bona fide' Western saloon with cowboys and cowgirls of all ages, sizes, and shapes, crowding the tables and bar.

Billie and Jolene, collectively advertised as 'The McPhail Sisters', are onstage at the far end of the room giving it big licks on a somewhat old-fashioned PA system.

At the other end of the room, perched on a bar stool, and aloof from the crowd, sits Cissie, a glass of once-sparkling water in front of her.

Billie and Jolene [*Together, sing*] 'Why does the world keep on turning? Why do the stars shine above? Don't they know it's the end of the world, it ended when I lost your love . . . I wake up in the morning and I wonder.'

Jolene takes an accordion solo.

Jolene [*Over music*] Don't look, Billie, but look who's proppin' up the far end of the bar.
Billie] Where? I cannae see . . . aw, yeh, I've spotted him.
Jolene] It's not a him, it's a her . . . Spotted who?
Billie] The guy with the speech impediment that wanted you an' I to go with him to Lourdes.
Jolene] Lourdes?
Billie] Aye . . . d'you not remember he came up to us in the Wells Fargo

an' he was walkin' all funny?
Jolene] Aw, wee Desmond, you mean? Don't talk daft, it wasnae Lourdes he wanted took, it was the loo, he'd got his galluses all twisted.
Billie and Jolene [*Onstage, sing*] ' . . . don't they know it's the end of the world, it ended when I lost your love.'

Billie and Jolene finish their song and their set, and leave the stage. There is a smattering of applause followed immediately by the clamour of conversation as the assembled 'cowpokery' return to their refreshments.

Billie] That went down well.
Jolene] 'Cos they never flang anythin'?
Billie] You don't want to push your luck an' do an encore, naw?
Jolene] Naw, I think we'll just hoof it for the hills . . . you didnae tell anybody who we were, did you?

At the other end of the room a tall cowpoke, with hands and forearms smothered in tattoos, edges up to the bar beside Cissie.

Tall Cowpoke] Howdy, Slim . . . *High Noon*, is it?

Cissie reacts with a blank stare.

Tall Cowpoke] All on your ownsome . . .
[*To barman*] Give us a big Glen Campbell, chief, an' whatever the little lady's huvvin'.
[*To Cissie*] Whit you fur, hen?

Cissie] I'm fine, thanks . . . an' we'll have less of the little lady.

Tall Cowpoke] Somebody give you a dizzy, yeh?

Cissie] Nobody gave us a dizzy, gonnae just vanish?

Tall Cowpoke] Now, that isnae what I'd cry 'neighbourly', honeybunch.

-TALL-COWPOKE-

Cissie] What you gonnae do, shoot me? I said I was fine . . . I'm fine, okay?

Tall Cowpoke [*Sotto voce, to barman*] Little lady's hud a dizzy . . . give it a coupla minutes an' bring us another big wanna these an' a Malibu, awright? Here . . .

He hands the barman a fiver.

Tall Cowpoke] . . . bung whatever's left over into the boattle fur the weans's wigwam party.

He picks up his glass and turns to Cissie.

Tall Cowpoke] 'Time was he supposed to be here at?

Cissie ignores him.

Tall Cowpoke] Eh?

Cissie continues to ignore him.

Tall Cowpoke] I guess you don't rightly know who I'm are, right?

Billie and Jolene have now started to pack up their gear by the side of the stage.

Jolene] Look, Billie, there' she's talkin' to Timberwolf Tierney, what d'you suppose she's bitin' *his* ear about?

Billie] Away over an' ask her.

Jolene] Naw, I couldnae, I'd be too . . . stop that, you.

Billie] She'll be orderin' up a set of louver doors, he's got them on special offer.

Jolene] How, what's up with them?

Billie] Same as what's up with all his stuff, they're all . . . [*Sniffs*] You been eatin' garlic?

Frank, Burberry buttoned up to the neck, makes his way backwards into the OK Korral bar from the street.
He turns, this way and that, spots Cissie and presses his way through the crowd towards her.

Tall Cowpoke] . . . an' that wan there wi' the daurk herr's 'Geronimo' . . .

He is giving Cissie a guided tour of his tattoos.

Cissie] What about that one with the pigtails an' the face like a burst tamatta . . . that wouldnae be Sittin' Bull, would it? Or have I got it wrong?

Tall Cowpoke] That's ma girlfriend.

Cissie] Whoops . . .

Tall Cowpoke] See, it's got it roon there at the tap . . . 'Roxanne' . . . boy took it affa Polaroid of her . . .

Cissie [*Quickly*] Naw, I'm sure it's a good likeness.

Tall Cowpoke [*Slowly*] Aye, it is.

He drains what's left in his glass.

Tall Cowpoke] Right, that's me . . . don't furget yur brochure . . . you'll fun yur dinette doors wi' yur prairie oyster motif on page two . . . ready-to-hang, fourteen quid. S'yur man handy wi' a hammer?

Frank slides up to the bar behind Cissie.

Frank] Don't turn around but guess who this is?

Tall Cowpoke] Better late than never, eh?

He gives Cissie a wink and takes off.

Cissie] I don't have to turn around, I got a whiff of the raincoat from two blocks away . . . what you doin' here? I thought you told me . . .

Frank] Yeh, but that was before Big Gordon OD'd . . . pretend you're not with me.

Cissie] I don't have to pretend . . .

She turns to face Frank.

Cissie] . . . who's Big Gordon?

Frank] 'The Boy Most Likely', Class of '68, St Saviour's High.

Frank turns away to try and catch the barman's eye.

Frank] . . . thought you said you didnae know anbody?

Cissie] Who, that geek that just left? Don't be . . .

Frank [*Interrupting*] God, these boots arenae half tight . . .

Cissie reaches down and lifts the tails of Frank's Burberry. He is wearing cowboy boots and Dorwood's Wranglers.

Frank] . . . yeh, okay, okay, I've decided to take on Dorwood's case.

He removes Cissie's hand and smooths down his raincoat.

Cissie] You've what?

Frank turns to face her.

Frank] Well, not take it on, exactly . . .

He takes a pair of Ray-bans from his raincoat pocket and puts them on.

Frank] . . . look closer into it, as you might say.

Cissie] What made you change your mind? Not that I'm not grateful, you understand . . . wasnae anythin' to do with Big Gordon, was it?

Frank] D'you ever catch the Hitchcock movie, *The Wrong Man*? Hank Fonda was in it . . .

The barman comes up and places a large malt whisky and a Malibu on the counter in front of them.

Barman] It's paid for, Stevie . . . Malibu's to your left.

Frank] Just saved me burstin' a ten-spot, Jim . . . [*To Cissie*] Played the bass fiddle in a night club orchestra.

He hands the Malibu to Cissie.

Cissie] Who . . . Big Gordon?

Frank picks up the whisky and sniffs at it.

Frank] Hank Fonda. This isnae funny, sweetheart.

Cissie] Penny's dropped, has it? Cheers.

She upends the glass and pours its contents on to the floor.

Over at the Bar-L David Cole in Ray Charles-type wraparound shades is seated at the Blüthner purveying Ray Charles-type wraparound R 'n' B.
    Fraser Boyle, in identical shades, is perched on a bar-stool by the piano, a tall glass clutched in his gloved fist.

David Cole [*Not looking at Boyle*] So what happened?

Boyle [*Not looking at Cole*] Nothin' happened . . . he wasnae in, was he?

David Cole] You didn't hang around?

Boyle] Just as well I never . . . another five minutes an' the joint was gonnae be hoachin' with SAS. Accordin' to my sources the guy's some kinda left-wing dev . . .

He breaks off as Shirley passes.

Boyle] . . . gonnae freshen that up for us, Gorgeous?

Shirley takes his glass.

Shirley] Mr Cole?

Cole shakes his head.
    Boyle waits till Shirley is out of earshot.

Boyle] 'Course, that's me all over, innit? Mr Trustin . . . the Gestapo's got his life story an' a full set of dabbities on file an' there's me swappin' pleasantries with the guy in the toilets.

David Cole] Yeah, what you gonna do 'bout my doors, man?

Boyle [*Interrupting, shouting at Shirley*] Ho, ask the fruitcake to go easy on the lemon scliffs, will you?

David Cole] Hey, I'm talkin' to you, meathead . . . you wrecked my goddam men's room, huh?

Boyle] Aye, awright, awright, I'll get my joiner to come over an' have a look-see, stop buggin' us about it, I've got enough on my plate with this missin' merchandise an' havin' to go round all my customers replicatin' their fish in a jotter!

David Cole] So what do I tell the Man from Motown when he calls?

Boyle] Just tell him everythin's cool, yeh?

David Cole] Everythin' better be cool 'cos this dude from Motor City don't mess with no amateurs, you know what I'm sayin'?

Boyle] You tell this dude not to fret himself, these people are pros . . . when the boys an' me met up with them in thon back room in Derry it wasnae just our side that were blindfolded . . . don't laugh, that was a gag. Believe me, there's nothin' amateur about these guys.

David Cole] I wasn't talkin' about those guys, stupid.

Boyle] Eh? Who were you talkin' ab . . .

Shirley [*Interrupting, loudly*] One Ball Breaker, plenty lemon scliffs!

She bangs the drink down in front of Boyle.

In the Lone Star Chinese restaurant in downtown Kilwinning Billie and *Jolene are seated in a booth scanning menus.*

Jolene] . . . Yeh, fine, but if we get the Lone Star Dinner-for-Three, an' the Cantonese Banquet over the page, we just need another two dishes an' you can wrap whatever beancurd you don't want in your neckerchief . . .

In the far-end booth Frank and Cissie are eating.

Frank] Cherokee what?

Cissie] Cherokee George . . . I've got his address in my bag . . .

Frank manipulates his chopsticks and manages to convey a single Singapore noodle to his mouth.

Cissie] . . . the only problem is you're gonnae have to get whatever lowdown he's got while you're in gettin' one done . . . d'you want that other pancake?

Frank] Help yourself . . .

He makes a note in his shorthand notebook open on the table.

Frank] . . . while I'm in gettin' one what done?

Cissie] A tattoo . . . pass me the Hoi Sin.

Frank [*Lookin up sharply*] What?

Cissie] The Hoi Sin sauce, you just put your elbow in it . . . Thanks.

Frank] I know this's goin' to strike you as wantonly perverse, given that I said I'd look into Dorwood's case, but I don't think I fancy gettin' a tattoo done . . . naw, cancel that . . . if I was asked what was the most obscene thing a human being could . . .

Cissie [*Interrupting*] It doesn't have to be anythin' elaborate.

She spoons some Hoi Sin sauce on to her pancake.

Frank] Aw, sure . . . coupla rattlesnakes an' 'Howdy, Stranger' across here in 'American Gothic' . . .

He draws his chopsticks across his forehead.

Frank] . . . in exchange for what, the name an' address of the nearest skin graft clinic?

Cissie] You're just bein' stupit now.

She arranges some cucumber and spring onion on a saucy pancake.

Frank] And you're bein' perfectly sensible, are you? S'up with me just takin' along a shorthand notebook an' askin' this Cherokee what's-his-name to . . .

Cissie [*Interrupting*] The guy isn't goin' to talk into a shorthand notebook, ya mutt . . . we're tryin' to infiltrate a closed community here . . . what d'you think I put you into camouflage for? Look, you don't imagine I'd ask you to go visit this party if I didn't reckon we were on to somethin'? Everybody that's anybody on the Country scene's been to Cherokee George, includin' Fraser Boyle, right?

Frank pours himself a glass of wine.

Frank] So?

He offers some wine to Cissie who refuses.

Cissie] So, it's like goin' to confessions to these dingbats, they all unburden themselves to their tattooist, don't they?

Frank] You tell me . . . I get the distinct impression I've just landed on Mars an' I've left my Baedeker in my other boilersuit.

Frank downs his glass and pours himself another.

Cissie] You remember that illustrated geek I was talkin' to in the OK?

Frank] The one you didnae know, yeh?

Cissie] I don't know him, he just came up an' started givin' me a guided tour of his torso . . . I gathered from him that . . . s'up?

You're not tellin' me you're chicken, are you?

She places some shredded duck on the pancake and rolls it up.

Frank] I'm not sayin' another dicky burd . . . how's your duck?

Cissie] My duck's awright.

She takes a bite out of the pancake.

Frank] 'Awright' is not an officially recognised Rab Haw rating . . . on a scale of one-to-ten, I'm talkin'?

Cissie ignores him.

Frank] A four, mebbe?

Cissie carries on munching.

Frank] Higher . . . lower?

He waits, pencil poised over his notebook.

Frank] C'mon, Crouch, I want to get this written up an' posted off to my editor . . . I might be on the run but I still have to earn a crust . . . a five, a two . . . what?

Cissie] You show me your bluebird, I'll let you know how I score the duck . . . right?

Frank] What blueburd?

Jolene [*Muffled, in the distance*] They want to get some Hoyt Axton on their hi-fi, that's hellish . . .

That same evening finds Frank leafing through a tattoo design catalogue. He is sitting in a dentist's chair, shirt sleeves rolled up, his Burberry hanging by the pay phone.

The tiny, unsalubrious backstreet tattoo parlour has peeling walls festooned with bleeding hearts, writhing snakes, and voluptuous mermaids. A thin layer of brownish grease has embalmed all surfaces.

Oriental tintinnabulation carries on in the background.

Frank] Naw, naw, they're very handsome, I was just wonderin' if you had somethin' a bit less . . . y' know?

Cherokee George] Bit less what?

The tattooist, Cherokee George, is in a filthy vest, with greasy pigtails, every inch of his exposed flesh is smothered in tattoos. He flips the page over.

Frank] Er . . . painful, really. Somethin' like a hummin' burd or a meadow pipit would be perfectly . . .

Cherokee George [*Leaning close*] Did you say 'meadow pipit'?

Frank] Okay, forget the meadow pipit . . . 'much is that one?

He points to a particularly gruesome group of vultures in the catalogue.

Cherokee George] Aw depends where you want it done, pal.

Frank] Up the Royal under a general anaesthetic, I would've thought.

Frank gives a little laugh.
Cherokee George remains stony-faced at this witticism.

Frank] You not got anythin' from the Disney archive I could look at?

Cherokee George] Disney?

Frank] 'Disney' matter . . . I'll come back another time when you're better dressed . . .

He makes to get up from the chair.

Cherokee George] I know your face from someplace, ya cheeky bastart.

He places a hand on Frank's chest.

Frank] D'you mind not doin' that, I'm an asthmatic . . . [*Coughs*]

Cherokee George] It wasnae the cages at Peterheid, was it?

Frank] Naw, it was livin' up a close in Possilpark, my whole family's got it . . . [*Wheezes loudly*]

Cherokee George] Who was it you said put you on to me?

He fixes Frank with his wall eye.

Frank] Aw . . . er . . . I don't think you'd know her . . . him, I

mean . . . Big Ted . . . Tex . . . Big Tex . . .

Cherokee George] Big Tex what?

Cherokee George puts his face next to Frank's and breathes on him.

Frank] . . . mebbe it was Wee Tex . . . yeh, come to think of it, he wasnae all that tall . . . in fact, I'm not all that sure his name was Tex, now that you mention it. Rex, naw? Lex? Yeh, that was it . . . Lex Somethin'. Or was it Rudy? Randy? Don't know any Randys, naw?

Cherokee George] I've definitely saw your face someplace . . . just cannae put ma finger on it.

Frank [*Interrupting*] Jody? Jesse? Wayne? Dwane? Clint?

George's eyes narrow.

Cherokee George] Did you say 'Dwane'?

Frank] Did I?

Cherokee George] Wasnae Dwane Devlin, was it?

Frank] Dwane Devlin . . .?

Frank snaps his fingers.

Frank] That's who it was . . . the Deadwood Playboys, right?

Cherokee George] Only your most decorated pedal-steel player in the business . . . aye, I done some of my best work on Dwane . . . s'a

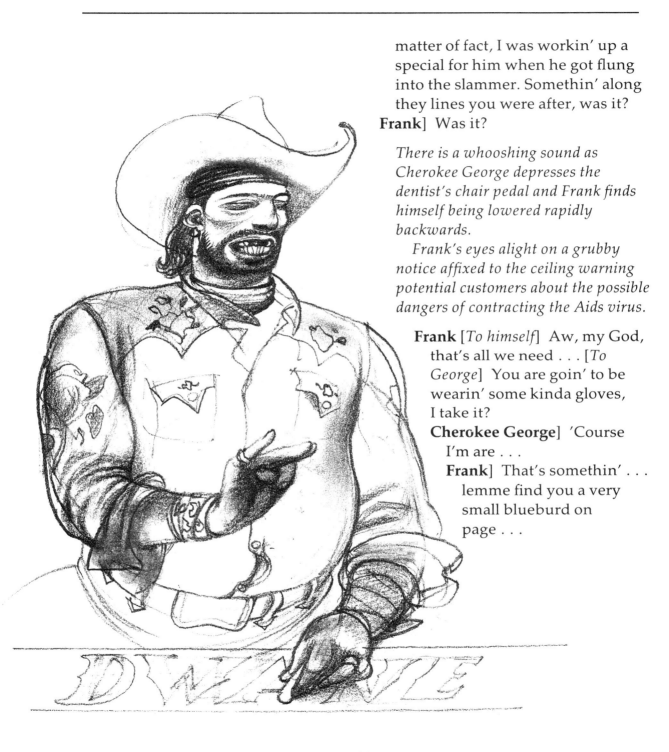

matter of fact, I was workin' up a special for him when he got flung into the slammer. Somethin' along they lines you were after, was it?

Frank] Was it?

There is a whooshing sound as Cherokee George depresses the dentist's chair pedal and Frank finds himself being lowered rapidly backwards.

Frank's eyes alight on a grubby notice affixed to the ceiling warning potential customers about the possible dangers of contracting the Aids virus.

Frank [*To himself*] Aw, my God, that's all we need . . . [*To George*] You are goin' to be wearin' some kinda gloves, I take it?

Cherokee George] 'Course I'm are . . .

Frank] That's somethin' . . . lemme find you a very small blueburd on page . . .

Frank flicks through the catalogue that he is still clutching.

Cherokee George] . . . freeze the gonads offa gopher in here.

He pulls on a filthy pair of fingerless Fair Isle gloves and uncorks a bottle of methylated spirits.

Frank] Naw, I'm sorry, that isn't quite . . .

Cherokee George [*Interrupting*] Page twenty-three.

He drenches a cotton wool swab with meths.

Frank] Page what?

He flicks through the catalogue.

Frank] Good grief.

Frank finds the page, he swallows in horror as he sees a picture of 'The Eagle of the Apocalypse in a Titanic Death struggle with the Sidewinders of Satan'.

Frank] Er . . . 'scuse me but I don't really think . . .

He is cut off in mid-sentence by the high-pitched whine of a tattooing 'gun'.

Cherokee George] Here, hold that a second . . .

He hands the tattooing 'gun' to Frank

and sets about securing him to the chair with a stout leather strap.

Frank [*Alarmed*] What you doin'?

Cherokee George] That's not too slack for you, naw?

Frank] Oooow!

Cherokee George takes the 'gun' from Frank.

Cherokee George] Better have a slug of this 'fore we get tore in, eh?

He tilts his head back and takes a swig from the meths bottle.

Frank] Aw, my God . . .

The Irish ferry is berthing at the Sealink terminal at Stranraer. Fraser Boyle, a pay phone to his ear, watches.

Boyle [*On phone*] . . . not that Bar-L, ya mug, this's a Yankee-style establishment I'm talkin' about . . . some vandal's put all their toilet doors in, I'm doin' the boy a favour . . . how quick can you . . . never heed what Roxanne wants to do, this's an emergency!

Cissie's apartment is a veritable shrine to 40s' and 50s' cowboy 'collectibles',

*most of which are in the process of
being wrapped up and packed into
tea-chests.*

*Cissie hands a steaming mug to
Frank who sits ashen-faced, his
Burberry draped around his
shoulders, his left arm in an
improvised sling.*

Cissie] Well?

Frank [*Shakily*] Give us a chance, I
havenae tasted it yet . . .

Cissie] You'll get that other arm in a
sling if you're not careful . . what'd
you find out, I'm askin'?

Frank] That I don't go a bundle on
guys with Red Indian nicknames
tyin' me up an' stickin' needles
into me, then chargin' sixty-five
quid plus VAT for the privilege,
but I could've told you that before I
went . . .

*He takes an exploratory sip from his
mug.*

Frank] . . . mmmm, Melrose's
Darjeeling, my very fav . . .

Cissie [*Interrupting*] It's Bovril, an' if
you don't hurry up an' tell me what
you discovered it's goin' straight
down the front of your Wranglers,
right!

Frank [*Indignantly*] Dorwood's
Wranglers . . . I wouldn't be caught
dead in a pair of . . .

Cissie] Hurry up, I said!

Frank] Aaaaaarg, my arm! Quit
shoutin' will you! D'you ever
hear . . . [*Lowers voice*] D'you ever
hear Dorwood talkin' about a
buncha guys callin' themselves . . .
God, what was it again?

Cissie] Callin' themselves what?

Frank] This is really aggravatin' . . . I
kept repeatin' it to myself all the
way here on the bus . . .

Cissie] Repeatin' what? C'mon.

Frank] . . . tch . . . it was on the tip of
my tongue, dammit . . . Somebody
Somebody and the Somethin'
Somethin' . . .

I told Cherokee what's-his-face I
was doin' a profile on the Playboys
for *Country Life* . . . an' I'd give his
tattoo parlour a plug if he filled in
some background detail on the
Deadwoods personnel for us . . .
which is when he brought up this
other buncha brainless bandits . . .
beg your pardon, this other
band . . .

*Meanwhile, back at the Sealink terminal
in Stranraer, Fraser Boyle flicks a
cigarette butt away as a convoy of
trucks disembarks from the ferry.
Boyle crosses the yard to the parked
fish van.*

As he does so a Winnebago with 'Jim Bob O'May and the Wild Bunch' lettered on the side rolls down the ramp and joins the convoy heading for the exit gate.

Boyle turns the key in the van's ignition and nudges his way into line behind the Winnebago.

In Cissie's apartment Frank is still wrestling with his memory.

Cissie] Forget about this other band, what'd he say about Fraser Boyle, ya dooley?

Frank] I'm comin' to that, I'm comin' to that . . . he seems to've been particularly palsy-walsy with Dwane . . . you havenae got a drink, have you?

Cissie] Dwane Devlin?

Frank] You know a lotta Dwanes, do you? An' you can cut the dooleys. I've just been through the most horrendous experience of my . . .

Cissie [*Interrupting*] Yeh, fine, just get on with it, hurry up.

Frank] Quit badgerin' us, I'm tryin' to collect my thoughts! This's bloody goupin'! Right, where was I?

Cissie] Rabbitin' on to no good purpose about some other band . . . will you get to the point, McClusky!

Frank] I'm gettin' to the point . . . if you'd chuck harassin' me for a second an' pin your ears back you might just latch on to the nub of this narrative!

Cissie] Don't shout!

Frank [*Loudly*] It's you that's shoutin'! Calm down . . . calm down . . . [*Calms down himself*] So, in bet . . . [*Clears throat*] So, in between beltin' down a half-litre of meths, workin' round my vaccination mark an' my polio injection, Cherokee what-d'you-call-him lets slip about how Boyle wasnae all that heartbroken when the other two band members got busted 'cos he, Boyle, had already got his marchin' orders from the Deadwoods an' was about to . . .

Cissie [*Interrupting*] Dorwood never mentioned that to me . . . carry on.

Frank] . . . an' was about to buddy-up . . . naw, sorry, I tell a lie . . his exact words were 'do a deal with' . . . and here I quote . . . 'a buncha bog-hoppin' badhats from the back-of-beyond called . . .'

Cissie] Called what?

Frank] . . . hold on, hold on!

He screws his eyes shut in a desperate bid to recollect their name.
    Cissie waits with bated breath.
    Frank opens his eyes.
    There is a deathly pause . . .

Frank [*Matter of fact*] Nup, it's away . . . gonnae chuck us a cushion? This arm isnae half . . .

Cissie rams a cushion at his back.

Frank] . . . ahyah!

Cissie] See you, you're hopeless . . . that's the last time you're gettin' sent for a tattoo!

In the Bar-L Timberwolf Tierney (aka Tall Cowpoke) adjusts his holster with its new hammer slung around his waist like a gunbelt and sniffs. His 'entourage' (apprentice, Drew, and girlfriend, Roxanne) lounge against the fittings awaiting instructions from their leader.

Tracey [*To Tall Cowpoke*] I'm just after tellin' you, the boss isnae here, he's went for a haircut . . . [*Loudly*] Shirley? You talk C 'n' W, come an' translate for us . . . [*To Tall Cowpoke*] . . . he's away gettin' scalped, yeh?

Cissie is trying to attend to Frank's wounds, but he shrinks away as she reaches out towards the dressing on his upper arm.

Cissie] Don't be a sap, I'm not goin' to hurt you . . . I just want to . . . look, we're not gonnae get very far if we don't trust each other . . .

Frank raises a skeptical eyebrow.

Cissie] Trust me, Frank . . .

Frank deliberates.

Cissie [*Softly*] . . . trust me.

Frank hesitates.
He looks into Cissie's eyes, and relaxes somewhat.

Frank] Awright, I trust you, but don't go an' . . . ooooooooooow!

Cissie peers at the spot on Frank's upper arm from which the dressing has been so untimely ripped.

Cissie] What is it?
Frank] That was bloody excruciatin', ya . . .! What d'you mean, what is it?

Cissie looks at a hideously discoloured and totally unidentifiable wound on Frank's upper arm.

Frank] It's the 'Eagle of the Apocalypse in a Titanic Death Struggle with the Sidewinders of Satan', innit!
Cissie] Aw, yeh . . . so it is.
Frank] Aw, God, I think I'm goin' to . . . bwoop.
Cissie] Here . . . hold this under your chin.

Frank grabs the proffered newspaper and runs to the bathroom.

Cissie [*Shouts*] An' don't use the wash-hand basin, d'you hear!

In a side-street in Candleriggs Boyle's fish van and Jim Bob's Winnebago are parked.
A motorcycle cop dismounts and starts slapping parking tickets on everything in sight.
In the Winnebago Boyle is talking to the Outlaw who is guarding Jim Bob's inner sanctum.

Boyle] Naw, hey, listen . . . tell Jim Bob I'll get him a 'taste' for later on the night an' he can let us know how much you guys want to order up for the European market . . .

The Outlaw carries on watching TV.

Boyle] . . . I had to return the sample

71

I had to my suppliers . . . wasnae just your top-notch quality, know what I mean?

The Outlaw turns a bloodshot eye on Boyle. Boyle sidles towards the door. The Outlaw goes back to watching Kind Hearts and Coronets *on his Sony as Boyle makes his exit.*

Boyle leaves the trailer and finds the motorcycle cop putting a ticket under the fish van's wiper.

Boyle [*To cop*] Ho, that fish motor's mine, I'm on a mercy dash to the Sick Children's Hospital with a loada cod liver oil capsules!

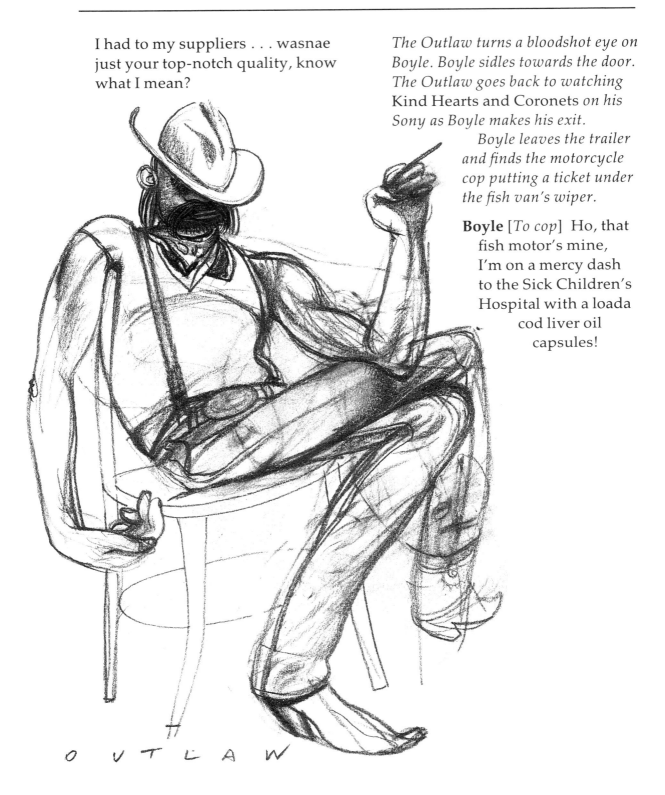

OUTLAW

In a fashion shop nearby Jolene, all in black, turns this way and that in front of a full-length mirror.

Jolene] Well, what d'you reckon?

Billie] I reckon it's about time we made some more phone calls, we're onstage at the Ponderosa the morra night an' we still havenae . . .

Jolene [*Interrupting*] Och, stop annoyin' us, there's a thousand guys'll jump at the chance.

Billie] We don't want a thousand, we just want a couple, Jolene.

Jolene] We'll get wurselves a couple, will you quit worryin' about it, Billie?

Billie] I cannae help worryin' about it, we're advertised on all the Wild Bunch posters as The McPhail Sisters and Friends, a right pair of numpties we're gonnae look turnin' up on wur tod.

Jolene] Speak for yourself . . . there's no way I'm lookin' a numpty.

Billie] Naw?

Jolene] What d'you mean, naw?

Billie] You seen the price that is?

Jolene] Where?

She examines the price ticket dangling from the hem of the blouson she is modelling.

Jolene] Good God, they're jokin'!

Billie] What about the wee guy that used to play with Big Norrie's Texas Handful? We could try givin' him a call.

Jolene shrugs off the overpriced blouson.

Jolene] Yeh, I suppose we could, but you'll need an awful lotta change . . .

She selects a green leather jacket from the rack.

Jolene] . . . he's in Tristan da Cunha with the Territorials . . . gonnae hold that for us?

Billie holds the leather jacket while Jolene slips her arms into its sleeves.

Billie] Okay, what about the guy with the stigmata that used to turn out all them tepee lampshades for Timberwolf Tierney's DIY shop, was he not quite an accomplished . . . awright, awright, scrub him. That leaves an amputee with an autoharp an' the big guy from Bearsden with the steel plate in his heid . . . let's face it, Jolene, the McPhail Sisters cannae come up with any Friends.

Jolene] Don't talk garbage, Billie, 'course we can.

Billie] Awright, name two . . . name one, you cannae.

Jolene] There's wee Desmond.

She strolls up and down in front of the mirror.

Billie] Jolene, wee Desmond cannae even say his own name right, we're talkin' about wur big chance here.

Jolene] Okay, how's about the boy MacIndoo?

Billie] MacIndoo?

Jolene] You forgot all about him, didn't you?

Billie] I sure did . . . who the hell's the boy MacIndoo?

Jolene] Don't tell me you don't remember the big fulla in the bi-focals that ran up all the bridesmaids' frocks for our Jinty's weddin'?

She executes a twirl.

Jolene] Him an' his pal used to front The Desperadoes . . .

Billie buries her face in the garment rack.

Jolene] . . . I'll get him to bring along your poncho.

Cissie is now clearing up her apartment and is wrapping cowboy memorabilia in sheets of newspaper and packing them into tea-chests.
The loo flushes.

Cissie [*Loudly*] There's a half-bottle of Listerine in the medicine cabinet . . . use it.

She picks up her Gene Autry radio and runs her fingers over its smooth bakelite contours.

Frank [*From bathroom*] Naw, it's okay, I washed my hair last Monday.

Cissie flicks the radio on and off, and then on again.
Jim Bob O'May's version of 'Your Cheatin' Heart' comes surging faintly forth before spluttering out.
Cissie turns the radio over and prises the back off with her fingernail.
In the bathroom Frank, looking pale, is already investigating the contents of the medicine cabinet and has come across a cracked snapshot of a smiling Cissie, Dorwood and a small child of about four in a cowboy suit.

Cissie [*From living-room*] D'you find it?

Frank looks at the photo for some moments.

Frank [*Loudly*] This'll be Dorwood junior, yeh?

Cissie's eyes widen in disbelief.

Frank [*From bathroom*] I said this'll be Dorwood junior, yeh?

Cissie [*To herself*] Aw, naw . . .

She withdraws a tightly-rolled bundle of twenty pound notes and then an avalanche of them tumbles out of the radio on to the carpet.

Back at George's tattoo parlour the sound of wheezy snoring can be heard while Jim Bob's 'Your Cheating Heart' plays over the radio. Cherokee George's manky socks are resting on the dentist's chair, there is a pair of discarded boots and an empty meths bottle on the floor.
The shop door rattles, and the unmistakable features of Fraser Boyle's face are pressed up against the glass panel.

Boyle] Right, ya dozy half-breed . . .

He takes a step away from the door and raises a boot.

The Tall Cowpoke is shaking his head while surveying the extensive damage to the cubicle doors of the Bar-L men's room.

Tall Cowpoke] Tch, tch, tch, tch . . . Drew, away oot tae the covered wagon an' get Roxanne tae start makin' oot some invoices . . .

He takes a hammer from his gunbelt and smashes at a door hinge.

Tall Cowpoke] . . . c'mon move yursel'.

His apprentice finishes blowing his nose on the roller towel and ambles across to the door.

Tall Cowpoke [*Shouts*] An' bring us a coupla lengths a timber . . .

The Tall Cowpoke takes a swing at the bottom hinge of a cubicle door, and it falls drunkenly on to the WC pedestal.

Tall Cowpoke] . . . thuv hud some bloody cowboy daein' thur carpentry fur them.

Frank is outside Cissie's apartment rattling the door handle.

Frank] Cissie? It's me . . . Frank . . . What you locked the door for? C'mon, I kept my side of the bargain . . . I want to know how you scored the duck. Cissie?

CHEROKEE · GEORGE ·

3

This Could Turn Septic on Us, Ya Big Ungrateful Midden

The rising moon over Barlinnie prison catches the bony contours of Dorwood Crouch's head, making him appear like an over-inked etching by Rembrandt.

Dorwood shuffles his way along the prison rooftop towards the shelter of a chimney stack, a cheap transistor radio clutched to his ear.

A loose slate skitters down the frosty pitch of the roof while Jim Bob O'May and the Wild Bunch's version of the Hank Williams classic 'Settin' the Woods on Fire', an upbeat anthem to incendiarism, fights a losing battle with the fading batteries.

★ ★ ★

Cissie chucks Frank's Burberry around his shoulders.

Frank] What's this?

Cissie] What does it look like?

Frank] It looks like a particularly roomy marquee but I can tell from the absence of guy ropes that it might just be my . . . where am I goin'?

Cissie] Home, where d'you think?

She escorts him to the front door of her apartment.

Frank] Thanks to you I no longer have a home, it's been ransacked . . .

Cissie opens the door.

Frank] . . . not to mention bein' put under surveillance ever since Big Gordon got fished out the Clyde . . . I'll have to find a bed an' breakfast joint an' lie low till all this blows over . . .

Cissie] Fine, I hope you'll be comfy.

Frank] That's it? I get myself indelibly lumbered with the 'Eagle of the Apocalypse', supply you with vital information concernin' Fraser Boyle an' a band whose name escapes me for the moment, the significance of which we've barely touched upon, an' all that's on offer is a not-so-hot Bovril and a decidely cool 'I hope you'll be comfy' . . . what is this?

Cissie] Yeh, that was a bit remiss . . .

Frank] I'll say it's remiss! Do you have any notion just how painful . . .

Cissie [*Interrupting*] . . . I hope you'll be very comfy, now beat it before I . . .

Frank [*Interrupting*] What the hell's got into you? Twenty-four hours ago you were on your bended knees beggin' me to look into Dorwood's case, to which end I've lost my apartment, shelved my better judgement, an' acquired a tattoo, now you cannae wait to get shot of me . . . no explanation, nothin'.

Cissie] What's to explain? You goofed . . . bye.

She gives Frank a shove and tries closing the door on him.

Frank] Ow! This could turn septic on us, ya big ungrateful midden!

Cissie [*Sotto voce*] Quit yelpin', will you! If it gets back to Dorwood that I've had a guy up the house he'll kill me!

Frank [*Interrupting*] Aw, I goofed awright . . . when I let you talk me into forkin' out sixty-five quid for this monstrosity when I could've got my motor outta . . . what d'you mean, I goofed?

Cissie] Screwed up . . . goofed . . . couldn't remember.

Frank] I'm still in a state of post-tattoo shock, for Christ's sake!

The elderly neighbour from upstairs shouts down.

Neighbour] Is that you, Mrs Crouch?

Cissie [*Sotto voce, to Frank*] See that. I told you to keep your voice down!

She hauls Frank back inside and closes the front door swiftly and silently.

Frank] What've I done now?

Cissie [*Interrupting*] Shhhhhhhhh!

Neighbour [*From upstairs*] Cooeeee?

Cissie presses a finger against her lips and herself against the wall.
    Some moments pass.

Frank [*Sotto voce*] She the one that shopped you to Dorwood that time?

Cissie [*Sotto voce*] In green biro, you want to've read the lies! He was nearly goin' off his head . . .

Frank] The old bastart!

Cissie] Told him I was goin' out with other guys while he was on remand.

Frank] An' were you?

Cissie gives him a kick on the shin.

Frank] Oooooooow!
Cissie] Shhhhhhhhhh!

Cissie places an ear against the door.

Cissie] She's still out there . . . listen.

Frank listens at the door.

Frank] I cannae hear anythin'.
Cissie] Listen!

They listen.
  There is complete and total silence.

Frank] Aw, yeh . . . a sort of low-decibel hum, right?

He moves his face closer to the back of Cissie's neck.

Frank [*Confidentially*] My old boy got one of them put in last Easter . . . four an' a half hours on the operatin' table . . . surgeon told my mother he was good for another ten years at least . . . gave up the ghost on the M90 two months back . . . passin' motorist tried to revive him with a set of jump leads an' a hockey stick but he was a gonner.
Cissie] Chuck that!
Frank] Naw, it's true . . . cross ma heart an' hope to . . .
Cissie [*Interrupting*] Not that . . . that!
Frank] What?

Cissie] Breathin' on me!
Frank] Anybody ever tell you what a beautiful . . . shhh!
Cissie] What?
Frank] Listen . . .
Cissie] Listen what! I cannae hear any . . .
Frank] Her pacemaker's either conked out or . . .

He hauls the door open.

Cissie] What're you doin'?
Frank] It's awright, she's away.
Cissie] Good, so are you . . . bye.

She shoves Frank out of the door on to the landing.

Frank] Ho, ya rotten big . . .!

And slams the door shut behind him.
  Frank tugs at his Burberry which is trapped in the door.
  He bends down and flips the letter box open.

Frank] Sixty-five quid plus VAT you owe me!

He turns to the neighbour who has appeared from upstairs.

Frank] Just delivered them a pizza . . . never even gave us a tip.

79

Dorwood sits, cold and dejected, hunched up against the chimney stack as the sporadic and feeble reception finally gives up the ghost and the transistor radio dies. He gives the radio a disgusted dunt, bangs it against the side of the chimney and then launches it high into the blackness.

A big red Chevrolet Drophead hoves into view, and draws up outside Bruno's Late Nite Barber Shop. David Cole, ultra-cool in his belted topcoat and shades, steps out.

Inside, Bruno's remains unaltered since the 1950s, right down to the row of latest hairstyles, 'Olympic', 'Tony Curtis', 'Blow-wave', 'Jeff Chandler', the Bush portable atop the Brylcreem dispenser, and Eric, whose name is spelled out on his overall pocket in red, and in stick-on plastic letters across the fly-blown mirror.

Eric's own favoured coiffure is a slightly-elevated 'Tony Curtis' that might easily be mistaken for a rug.

Jim Bob's 'Settin' the Woods on Fire' carries on over the radio.

Eric swoops low for a final snip at the back of a customer's head.

David Cole enters, unbelts his topcoat, and hangs it up as the final chords of 'Settin' the Woods on Fire' fade on the Bush portable.

Eric holds up a two-handed mirror and his customer in the chair nods his approval.

Radio DJ] . . . Jim Bob O'May and the Wild Bunch there with a sizzling cut from their *Lean 'n' Tasty* album . . . seventeen minutes past the hour . . .

Eric plucks the towel from his customer's shoulders and gives it a shake.

The customer gets up from his chair, still wearing a barber's sheet.

As the customer and David Cole pass, Cole slips a package to him in exchange for some folded banknotes.

Cole takes his place in Eric's chair.

The customer removes the sheet and passes it to Eric who throws it over Cole and tucks the corners into the back of his collar.

Radio DJ] . . . no need to remind Jim Bob fans that the boys are back in town on the first leg of a European Tour that kicks off in Wishaw tomorrow night, with local support act The McPhail Sisters and Friends, before heading up country to Aberdeen . . .

E   R   I   C

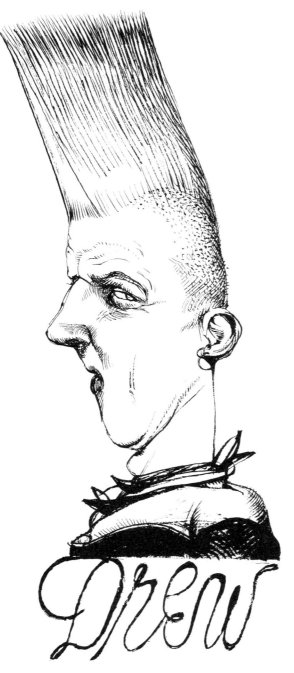

Across town, in the Bar-L men's room, a grubby ghetto-blaster is tuned to the same radio station.

Radio DJ] . . . you're tuned to *The Old Chisholm Trail* on 289 metres . . . six pairs of those Wild Bunch tickets to be won in our great phone-in competition directly after the news headlines from Ward Ferguson . . .

The Tall Cowpoke emerges from the end cubicle.

Radio News Reader] . . . Cheers, Dunky . . . and we go straight over to the radio car and *Evening Echo* reporter, Tamara MacAskill, for an update on the rooftop protest at HM Pris . . .

The Tall Cowpoke stabs at the off button.

Tall Cowpoke] How we daein', young Drew?

Drew] Jist drivin' hame this last . . .

There is a loud hammering.

Drew] . . . screwnail.

Drew emerges from another cubicle and pulls its door shut behind him.
The replacement door with its high-gloss finish and Western-style pokerwork decoration doesn't quite

manage to close properly.

The other cubicle doors, with the exception of the not-too-badly-damaged original end door, have been patched or nailed over with hardboard sheeting, and are slightly at odds with the badly-hung replacement door and the art deco surroundings.

The apprentice joins the master as they assess their handiwork.

The Tall Cowpoke takes the hammer from Drew and slips it into his 'gunbelt'.

Tall Cowpoke] Coupla coats a dark stain an' I defy embody tae spot the difference . . .

Drew stabs a black-nailed finger at the ghetto-blaster 'on' button.

Tamara] . . . between the shower block and the prison laundry.

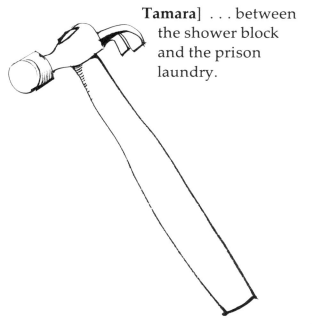

As the radio news reporter speaks into her in-car microphone, under the prison wall, Dorwood totters unsteadily along the apex of the roof high above.

Tamara] No attempt has been made so far this evening to bring the man down owing to the treacherous conditions on the roof . . .

Dorwood's foot slips on the frosty slates and he teeters for a moment before regaining his equilibrium.

Tamara] . . . but prison authorities are expected to move in at first light to help de-escalate what could very well be a repetition of the violent rooftop demonstrations we saw earlier in the year at a number of Scottish institutions . . . a spokesman for the Governor assured journalists just before we came on air that every effort is being made to contact the prisoner's wife who is thought to be still living at the couple's luxury maisonette in Clydebank . . . Tamara MacAskill for Radio Kelvin News, Riddrie.

Tamara leans down to the radio car window.

Tamara] Brian . . . d'you fancy a quick coffee or d'you think we should hang around in case he plunges to his death? I'm easy . . .

★ ★ ★

Frank is still standing outside Cissie's front door. He can hear the telephone ringing inside.

Frank] The very least you could do is phone us a taxi . . .

He tugs at the trapped Burberry.

Cissie [*From inside*] There's a box at the corner.

The telephone keeps on ringing.

Frank] Yes, positively rib-tickling . . . how d'you expect me to dial for a taxi with this!

He waves his sling at the door.

Cissie [*From inside*] Get a bus!

Frank] Aw, first class . . . you know fine well I cannae risk usin' public transport with my face plastered all over the papers every Tuesday and Friday!

He tugs fiercely at his Burberry, and there is a ripping noise.

Cissie [*At letterbox*] Stop exaggeratin', your own mother wouldn't recognise you from that photograph . . .

Her fingers appear through the letterbox.

Cissie] . . . it's this big.
Frank] That big!

The telephone stops ringing.

Frank] 'Much d'you want to bet that was my Features Editor? I'm supposed to be at a sushi restaurant in East Kilbride right now!

★ ★ ★

Fraser Boyle stands in Cherokee George's tattoo parlour stamping up and down and blowing into his hands, his breath steaming in the icy atmosphere.
There is the sound of running water.

Cherokee George] What'd you say?

Cherokee George lifts his head out of the sink, his teeth chattering, groping for a towel.

Boyle] I said, I've tried everyplace . . . soon as you mention Cole they don't want to know . . . God, it's bloody chitterin'.

Cherokee George] You're no' kiddin' . . . freeze the gonads . . .
Together] . . . offa gopher in here.
Boyle] Aye, very apt . . . so what time does your guy normally deliver at?
Cherokee George] What guy?

George stops drying his hair and looks up from under the towel.

Boyle] What guy . . . your supplier! What d'you suppose I kicked the door in for, I've ran out, haven't I!
Cherokee George] Awright, awright, hing loose . . . you should've kicked it in a bit earlier, I'm no' that long off the phone to his missus . . . God, ma heid . . .

Boyle snatches the pay-phone from the wall.

Boyle] Here . . . tell her you want another six bags . . .

George takes the phone.

Boyle] . . . c'mon, I've got people waitin' for us!

George sticks his finger in the dial.

Cherokee George] Better have some readies on you, this boy doesnae take cards or nothin' . . .
Boyle] Get a move on, it's freezin'!
Cherokee George] Six, did you say? [*To phone*] Aye, hullo, George

Tierney here . . . could you ask your man to stick another six bags on to that order, love?

Boyle] An' it better no' be cut with nothin' or you're for it.

Cherokee George [*On phone*] Hold on . . . [*To Boyle*] D'you want any logs, she's askin'?

Boyle's expression changes.

Boyle] Logs? What you talkin' about, logs?

Cherokee George [*To phone*] Naw, jist the Grade One Smokeless, darlin' . . . ta.

He hangs up.

Cherokee George] Be here at the back a nine, he's got four ton a nuggets to drop off at the Blind Basket showrooms . . .

He drops the towel over his face and starts drying his hair.

Cherokee George] What?

George lifts the towel from his head just as Boyle's fist comes crashing into it.

Frank hunches morosely in the back of a taxi, his Burberry draped over his shoulders, nursing his tattooed arm.

Billie [*On radio*] Car Fourteen to base . . . come in base, over? [*Over shoulder to Frank*] Jolene said it was a lassie's voice that phoned . . . good job for you it was dark.

There is a short eruption over the radio.

Billie [*On radio*] Yeh, Jolene . . . let your fingers do the walkin' . . . B an' Bs, South Side, over? [*To Frank*] This you gettin' evicted, yeh?

Frank] Naw, this is not me gettin' evicted . . . shuttup.

Billie] What's the long face for . . . well?

Frank] I wasnae aware I had a long face.

Billie] Any longer an' you could tuck it into your underpants . . . somebody die, yeh?

Frank] Not yet but there's still time . . . give it a rest, will you?

Billie] There's definitely somethin' up. I can tell . . .

There is another unintelligible interruption over the radio.

Billie [*On radio*] Naw, B an' Bs, Jolene . . . YMs, one-star hotels, flop-houses, over. [*To Frank*] Is it your kidneys, mebbe?

Frank] Is what my kidneys?

Billie] Made you go that funny colour?

Frank] What funny colour?

Billie] Like a peely-wally satsuma.

Frank] Aw, yeh, thanks, that's cheered me up no end, that has. If you must know, I've just had myself tattooed . . . awright?

Billie] Tattooed?

Frank] Yeh . . . tattooed!

Billie] What with, your name an' address in case you turn up lost again?

There is an incomprehensible message over the radio.

Billie [*On radio*] S'that includin' all the ones over the page, over.

There is a short response.

Billie [*On radio*] Naw, put your phone down . . . d'you want to try . . . lemme think . . . d'you want to try . . .?

Frank] They cannae all be full up, surely to God?

Billie [*On radio*] I'm puttin' you on hold, Jolene . . . [*To Frank*] Did you say somethin'?

Frank] I said, there has to be one that has a vacancy, naw?

Billie] One what? [*On radio*] You still on hold, Jolene, over?

Frank] One of the boardin' houses . . . s'that not what you were talkin' to her about?

Billie] Her?

Another short eruption over the radio.

Frank] Her on the walky-talky.

Billie] If it's any of your business, which I venture it isnae, 'her' on the walky-talky an' I happen to be discussin' the chances of comin' up with a coupla sidemen, at short notice, to help beef out the McPhail Sisters' lineup when me an' Jolene . . .

Frank] The McWho Sisters?

Billie] . . . when me an' Jolene go out on this mini-tour with Jim Bob O'May an' . . .

Frank] . . . The Wild Bunch! Yahoooooooo, that's it!

Billie [*Coldly*] Yahoo, that's what?

On the prison roof Dorwood is attempting to roll a cigarette in the cold and windy conditions.

Tamara is shouting to him from the street below.

Dorwood [*Loudly*] C . . . I . . . double S . . . [*To himself*] damn an' bugger it. [*Loudly*] . . . I . . . E!

Tamara [*Shouting*] D'you want me to give her a message?

Dorwood [*Loudly*] What?

Tamara [*Shouting*] Any message?

Dorwood [*Loudly*] Naw, just tell her I

want to see her . . . I don't trust these animals.

Tamara leans down to the car window.

Tamara [*To engineer*] Did you manage to get that address, Brian?

Dorwood [*Loudly from the roof*] Ask her to bring us two hunner Bensons an' somethin' to eat, the grub in here's diabolical!

Tamara] What's he wittering on about now?

Engineer] They want to get a marksman out here an' pick the bugger off . . .

Tamara [*Shouting*] I'm sorry, I can't hear you!

Engineer] I said, they want to get a police marksman out here . . .

Dorwood [*Loudly*] There's my redundancy money off the rigs inside the Gene Autry wireless, tell her.

Tamara leans down to the car again.

Tamara [*To engineer*] Something about Jean, is that what you got?

Engineer] He's just after tellin' us the wife's name was Cissie, what one we supposed to bring back, the wife or the fancy wumman?

Dorwood [*Loudly*] I was savin' up to take her an' . . . I was savin' up to take us to Nashville, if she asks you.

Billie's taxi is parked outside Cissie's apartment block, the radio continues to give out incomprehensible messages.
Billie is leaning against the cab, mike in hand.

Billie [*On radio*] Say again, over?

There is a burst of static in reply.

Billie [*On radio*] Naw, Jolene, forget about the B an' Bs, I'm back at the pick-up point with Rab Haw gettin' to grips with this other business, over.

Cissie and Frank are both slumped on the back seat in the darkened interior of the taxi. Cissie has a coat pulled over her nightclothes.

Cissie] Are you actually tellin' me this's what you chapped me up for?

Billie [*On radio*] Naw . . . 'Haw' . . . as in 'Haw, you', over.

Cissie] I've never heard anythin' more ridiculous in my life . . .

The static continues.

Frank [*Interrupting*] I told her you wanted to be billed under your maiden name.

Billie [*On radio*] Hold on I'll ask . . .

Cissie] You don't even know my maiden name . . . bloody cheek!

Billie's head appears through the window.

Billie [*Interrupting, to Frank*] Jolene wants to know what outfits you've played bottleneck for an' how come her an' I's never heard of any them?

Cissie] Och, I'm away back to my bed . . .

She climbs out of the taxi.

Frank [*To Billie*] Just tell Jolene that Ry Cooder's got my home number an' I've got his, okay?

He clambers out of the taxi after Cissie.

Frank [*To Cissie*] Hoi, come back here . . .

Cissie stops to retrieve her slipper.

Billie [*On radio*] You there, Jolene, over?

Frank catches up with Cissie.

Frank] It's not any more ludicrous than you askin' me to go visit Cherokee Georgie Boy . . .

Cissie] Yeh, it is.

Frank] . . . you've done it before.

Cissie] Scab off.

Frank catches her by the arm.

Frank] Listen, I didn't go through hell gettin' this on my arm just so I could wake up handcuffed to the bedpost in some crummy roomin' house with Gordon Smart on my conscience . . . stop actin' the . . .

Cissie] Scab off, I said!

She pulls away from him.

Frank] . . . stop actin' the prima donna! If you were serious about helpin' you-know-who you wouldn't hesitate . . .

Cissie [*Interrupting*] If you're referrin' to Dorwood why don't you . . .

Frank clamps his free hand over Cissie's mouth.

Frank [*Sotto voce*] Shhhhhhhh, d'you want to blow it! If the McWhat-d'you-call-them Sisters get wind that joinin' their band's just an excuse for a covert operation we'll get the bum's rush . . . as far as they're aware, I'm a Chet Atkins playalike with an NUJ card an' you're just some dumb outta-work waitress that used to yodel a bit with the Tumblin' Driftwoods, let's keep it like . . . ooooooow!

He withdraws his hand from Cissie's mouth with a set of her teethmarks on it.

Cissie] Driftin' Tumbleweeds an' that was ten years back . . . what makes you think I'm all that desperate to get back onstage an' start apein' Tammy Wynette!

Frank] You don't have to ape Tammy Wynette, just doll yourself up an' I'll cover for you . . . you want to get the dope on Fraser Boyle an' clear Dorwood's name, don't you?

Cissie turns away.

Frank] Well, don't you?

Cissie] Look, there's somethin' I really ought to tell you . . .

Frank] What? Naw, lemme guess . . . you're chicken, right?

Cissie turns to face Frank.

Cissie] What'd you say?

There is a short eruption over the radio.

Billie [*On radio*] . . . naw, I reckon she would be hunky-dory, it's wur slide-guitar picker I'm still a bit dubious about . . . he's only got the one . . .

Frank [*Loudly*] Aaaahyah!

Billie [*On radio*] . . . as you were, Jolene . . . lemme check if he doubles on mouth harp, over.

Tracey is peering curiously through the Bar-L men's room door.

Tracey [*To occupants*] . . . it's awright, I'm just lookin' . . .

She withdraws her head and closes the door.

Tracey] . . . aw, my God . . .

Shirley passes on her way to the kitchen.

Shirley] Don't tell me, they've left the joint a shambles?

Tracey] Have a gander.

She holds the door open again. Shirley hesitantly steps forward to have a peek.

Shirley [*To occupants*] It's awright, I'm just look . . . aw, my God . . . The big guy's gonna do his nut!

A grimy Mercedes, with a bashed-in front fender, pulls up outside Bruno's barber shop and stops behind David Cole's car. Three men get out.

The driver leans against the bonnet while his two companions, one limping and one, a short man called Tonto in a baggy check suit, go into the shop.

Eric glances up from razor-stropping as the bell above the front door jangles.

Jim Bob O'May and the Wild

Bunch's version of 'It Keeps Right On A-Hurtin' plays over the radio.

The limping man and the short man pull their balaclava masks down over their faces and the limping man eases himself down on to a bentwood chair, his gammy leg stuck out in front of him.

David Cole, with hot towels covering his face, is unaware that anything untoward is going on.

Eric carries on stropping.

The short man rolls up his companion's right trouser leg. Strapped to the limping man's leg with broad strips of adhesive tape is a sawn-off shotgun. The short man starts to remove the tape, but the limping man indicates that he will remove the rest of the tape himself.

The short man crosses to the mirror and picks up a shaving mug and brush.

Eric carries on stropping.

The short man works up lather in the mug.

The limping man, sawn-off shotgun in one hand, is trying to rid his other hand of the tiresome tape.

The short man crosses the room and relieves the limping man of the unwanted tape, and is now lumbered with both shaving mug and tape.

The limping man waves the shotgun at Eric.

The short man crosses to Eric who relieves him of the tape. Eric slices at the tape with the razor. The tape promptly sticks to the razor and won't come off.

The limping man now crosses to the Bush portable and turns the volume up.

David Cole [*From under towels*] Hey, c'mon, what's with the loud music, man?

The music carries on.

David Cole [*Loudly*] Whatsamatter, you deaf or . . .

There are sounds of a scuffle under the closing bars of the record.

David Cole feels hands on his towels.

David Cole] . . . git that thing outta ma face, what the hell you doin'?

Radio DJ] . . .the Wild Bunch and 'It Keeps Right On A-Hurtin'', and that comes with special birthday greetings for seven-year-old Trento Capaldi of Bishopbriggs who'll be nine this coming Friday . . .

There is a deafening shotgun blast, and pink shaving foam splatters the radio.

Radio DJ] . . . four pairs of fabulous Jim Bob tickets still up for grabs as we go back to the phone-lines . . .

91

★ ★ ★

Billie's taxi is still parked outside Cissie's apartment block. The radio is now tuned to the Country music station.

Radio DJ [*Over radio*] . . . who's on line one?

Frank walks towards the taxi and opens the passenger door and climbs into the back seat.

Radio DJ] Line two? Anybody on line two? Okeydokey, we'll go to line three . . . are you there, line . . .

Billie flicks the radio off.

Billie] Well, what's the verdict?
Frank] Jury's still out.
Billie] Meter's still runnin'.

★ ★ ★

Meanwhile the radio car is prowling the streets nearby with Tamara and the radio engineer inside.

Tamara [*Into carphone*] D'you want to read that back, Trish?

Tamara peers out of the car window at the passing houses.

Tamara [*To engineer*] D'you remember what number he said? [*Into carphone*] That should be 'robbery' not 'rubbery', Trish.

Engineer] I don't know what you're botherin' for, bugger'll be tucked up in his cell wi' the latest Hank Jansen right now . . .

Tamara [*Into carphone*] No . . . colon, dash, new para.

Engineer] . . . five years in the forces, that's what they want to give these wastrels . . .

Tamara [*Into carphone*] Right, thanks, Trish . . . get them to send out a photographer . . . bye.

She replaces the phone.

Engineer] . . . army sniper wi' an M16 would've saved us all this trouble.

Tamara] There it is . . . 'Campsie Quadrant'.

The carphone bleeps.

Engineer [*Into carphone*] Meals On Wheels, yes?

Tamara] If you turn left just here, Brian . . .

Engineer [*Into carphone*] What d'you want?

Tamara] . . . no, left . . . left. You've driven right past it.

Engineer] Forget it, you've got an appointment at the hairdresser's.

He hands the carphone to Tamara.

Tamara] Hairdresser's?

Billie and Frank are still sitting in her taxi outside Cissie's apartment block.

Billie] Right, you ready? This's your starter for ten . . .

She consults some notes on her lap. Frank sticks his head out of the window as the radio car speeds past. He watches it disappear down the street.

Billie] . . . you're on your own, no conferring . . . who wrote the 1955 Tennessee Ernie hit, 'Sixteen Tons'?

Frank] I could be wrong, but was that not Tamara MacAskill?

Billie] Naw, Merle Travis . . . that's ten points to me. Who wrote . . .

Frank] It's me to go . . . Who wrote *Mein Kampf*? Picture clue . . . it's a book.

Billie] Er . . .

Frank] Must hurry you . . .

Billie] Vangelis?

Frank] No, Hitler. Who wrote 'Oh, Lonesome Me'?

Billie] Don Gibson!

Frank] Naw, not that 'Oh, Lonesome Me', the other one . . . d'you give in?

Billie [*Indignantly*] There wasnae another one.

Frank] 'Fraid there was, Shorty . . . George Stafford . . . came ninth in the egg an' spoon at St Saviour's Sports . . . scratched it on the back of Libo Ragazzo's neck, two verses an' a chorus. Big tall guy with no eyebrows . . . his old lady was a beachcomber . . .

There is a rap at the steamed-up passenger window.

Frank] . . . wasnae a hit, mind you.

He slides the window down. Cissie stands there hugging herself in the cold.

Frank [*To Cissie*] Yes?
Cissie] We need to talk.
Frank] I'm right in the middle of a quiz.
Cissie] We need to talk now.

Frank looks at Billie.

Billie] You heard.

Frank climbs out of the taxi.

Frank] So talk.
Cissie] Not here . . .

She takes his arm and leads him off along the street.

Cissie] . . . you know when you were in the bathroom?
Frank] Throwin' up, yeh?
Cissie] Please . . .

Frank] I forgot to screw the top back on the Listerine bottle.

Cissie] This's serious!

Frank] Ow!

Cissie] D'you remember that Gene Autry wireless . . .?

Frank] Do I remember that Gene Autry wireless what . . . profile . . . documentary . . . request show . . . what?

Cissie [*Interrupting*] We've got a Gene Autry wireless . . . radio . . . bakelite . . . about this size . . . 1949 . . . Dorwood bought it off one of the roustabouts up in Aberdeen for eighty-seven quid.

Frank] S'that a bargain, yeh? I mean, I don't know about these things.

Cissie] I'm not talkin' about whether it was a bargain or not, I'm talkin' about what was inside the bloody thing!

Frank] You mean, like valves an' stuff? [*Shakes head*] You don't mean like valves . . .

Cissie] Eighteen thousand quid, I've just counted it.

Frank] An' it cost how much, eighty-seven? Sounds like a bargain to me, Crouch.

Cissie] You know what this means, don't you?

Frank] Er . . . [*Ponders*] Christ, this's worse than *University Challenge* . . . lemme think, lemme think . . .

Cissie] Somebody hid it there, ya dummy!

Frank] Ah, right, I'm with you now . . . the roustabout was usin' it as a piggy bank an' you've mislaid his address so you cannae . . . ow! Chuck punchin' us!

Billie [*Shouting out of taxi window*] Okay, what's the score . . I've got Jolene screamin' over the radio at us . . . you doin' it or you not doin' it?

Fraser Boyle is still pacing around the tattoo parlour, waiting while Cherokee George listens into the telephone.

Cherokee George] Better have some ready cash on you, this boy doesnae take cards or nothin' either . . .

Boyle puffs on a cigarette.

Boyle [*Irritably*] I've got ma fish money . . . get on with it!

Cherokee George] . . . six, did you say?

He turns his head to address Boyle, his blackened eye shining.

Cherokee George [*On phone*] Aye, hullo, Indian Love Call here . . . I've got a client that's severely in need of a six-pack urgent . . .

Boyle] An' it better no' be cut with nothin' or you're for it.

Cherokee George [*On phone*] Hold on . . . [*To Boyle*] Where d'you want him to make the drop? No' here, I've got the coalman comin' . . .

Boyle] Ask him to meet up with us at . . .

Cherokee George] What about the Cactus Club? He knows where that is . . .

Boyle] Aye, an' so does every narc in the city . . . tell him to make it the Bar-L.

Cherokee George] That no' a bit tactless? Boy just got paroled last Wednesday there . . .

Boyle] No' that Bar-L, ya clown . . . the noo pianna bar in the old ice-cream works . . . I'll be there in twenty minutes, tell him.

He moves towards the door.

Cherokee George [*On phone*] Hullo, you still there, Tonto?

Fraser Boyle appears in the doorway of the tattoo shop. A large sheet of crumpled cardboard covers the broken glass panel which Boyle kicked in.
  Boyle shivers, turns up his jacket collar, sticks his hands into his jacket

pockets and hurries off to where the fish van is parked.
  A few moments later, Cherokee George appears. He looks up and down the street.

Cherokee George [*To himself*] Aw, brilliant . . . how they supposed to recognise wan another?

He has another look up and down the street before going back inside the parlour and slamming the door.
  A few moments later, he reappears. He checks busted door panel.

Cherokee George] An' I'm doin' this guy a favour?

He shakes his head in incomprehension.

Cissie is slumped on the floor of her apartment in front of the empty fireplace, her eyes glued to the TV with the sound turned down.
  On the screen Dorwood, Dwane, and Fraser Boyle play and mouth the words to 'Your Cheatin' Heart'. At the end of the song Dorwood slips off his Dobro, hands it to Boyle, and crosses to talk to Jonathan Ross on The Last Resort *set.*
  The doorbell rings.
  Cissie continues watching TV.
  The doorbell rings again.

Neighbour [*From landing*] Are you there, Mrs Crouch?

*Cissie struggles to her feet, crosses to the living-room door, and closes it.
   The doorbell rings again.*

Neighbour [*From landing*] Mrs Crouch?

Cissie hits the rewind button on her video commando, spools back, and turns up the volume on the Deadwood Playboys' 'Your Cheatin' Heart'.

*On the Barlinnie Prison rooftop Dorwood stares intently at a snapshot of a child. He runs his thumb across the photo.
   He sits crouched against a chimney stack with the distant 'whoop-whoop' of police cars in the air around him.*

In a street nearby the Tall Cowpoke, Drew and Roxanne are driving in their 'covered wagon' as police cars and an ambulance, blue lights flashing, rush past them in the opposite direction.

Tall Cowpoke] 'Much d'you want tae wager that's some stupit wean goat its heid stuck in the palin's?

*Fraser Boyle's fish van pulls up short outside the Bar-L Piano Bar, Boyle jumps out and clamps a pair of wraparound shades to his face despite the darkness.
   Inside, Spencer the barman is preparing a cocktail.
   Shirley and Tracey rush to and fro with orders.*

Tracey [*To Shirley, en passant*] Some long haircut the big guy's gettin', is it not?

Fraser Boyle enters from the street and crosses to the bar.

Boyle [*En route, to Tracey*] Ho, do us a favour, Gorgeous, there's somebody gonnae be lookin' for us . . .
Tracey] You're not kiddin' . . . do yourself a favour an' beat it before he gets here . . .

She moves on to serve at a banquette.

Tracey [*To diners*] Who's the Gumbo?

Boyle carries on to the bar.

Boyle [*To Shirley*] Ho, do us a favour, Gorgeous, there's somebody gonnae be lookin' for us only I'm no' too sure they know . . .

Shirley [*Interrupting*] You said it, bub . . . I'd make myself scarce, if I was you . . . he'll be here any minute. [*To Spencer*] Two club sodas, one tequila.

Boyle [*To himself*] What is this? [*To Spencer*] 'Scuse me, pal, there's somebody gonnae be lookin' for us only I'm no' too sure they know who I'm are . . .

Spencer] Aw, I'm pretty positive they do . . . don't worry, I'll bring you some grapes.

Boyle [*To himself*] Call it paranoia but there's somethin' funny goin' on here . . .

Shirley moves off with some drinks and Tracey passes the bar on her way to the kitchen.

Tracey [*To Boyle*] You still here . . . God, you're no' feart.

Boyle [*To Spencer*] Have you had a call from a dozy half-breed, by any chance?

Spencer [*Loudly*] Shirley . . . have we had a call from a dozy half-breed?

Boyle] Soon as I've been to the toilet somebody's for a doin' . . .

He heads off towards the men's room.

The street outside Bruno's Late Nite Barber Shop is cordoned off with

uniformed police officers stationed outside the scene of the crime.

Plain-clothes men are dusting a big American car for prints, while others are ferrying plastic bags from the shop to a police van.

Tamara MacAskill is filing her radio report.

Tamara] . . . the man leading the murder inquiry, Chief Inspector Docherty of Strathclyde Regional Crime Squad, did make a brief statement to reporters a few minutes ago but declined to name the victim of this brutal and apparently motiveless crime . . .

Tamara stands, mike in hand, a few yards from the radio car.

Behind her, two ambulance men carry a bodybag to the waiting ambulance.

Tamara] . . . I have with me, however, an eye-witness, Mr . . .

Eric] . . . Eric.

Tamara] . . . Eric Tierney . . . tell me, Eric . . .

Eric leans into the mike.

Eric] I never seen nothin'.

Tamara] . . . I believe you were actually on the premises when the two men . . .

Eric [*Interrupting*] I never seen nothin' but I'd like to say hullo to my elderly mother in ward ten at Stobhill Hospital . . .

Police Sergeant [*Approaches, gesticulating*] Haw, you . . . bawheid . . . get you back in this vehicle!

Tamara [*To Eric*] . . . you did say, did you not, that one of the killers had what you describe as a 'Fats Domino-type' accent, is that correct?

Eric] Naw, hen, that was the big fulla that got his face blew off his heid . . .

He leans close to the mike again.

Eric] . . . if you're listenin' to this on your headphones, Ma, I want you to know that I'm awright an' that George and Tommy'll be up on Thursday wi' your gift tokens . . .

The police sergeant appears at Tamara's side.

Police Sergeant] Right, miss, you an' the crew back into the motor an' bugger off . . . c'mon, shift yourself!

He starts hustling her towards the radio car.

Tamara [*Into mike*] I am now being forced backwards towards the radio car but not before I've had a chance to ask Mr Tierney if . . .

Eric [*Loudly*] I never seen nothin'.

Police Sergeant [*To Eric*] Get you into that van an' keep your mouth shut or you're for a sore face, m'boy.

Tamara [*Loudly*] . . . Tamara MacAskill, for Radio Kelvin's *Crime Beat* . . . Tobago Street. [*Off-mike*] Stop pushing, ya big shite!

The radio is on inside Billie's taxi.

Radio DJ] And we'll be rejoining *Evening Echo* reporter, Tammy MacAskill, later in the show for more news on that sensational barber shop slaying . . .

Frank reclines in the back seat of the taxi, his eyes closed.

Radio DJ] . . . five minutes to the top of the hour on the Dunky Chisholm show . . . two pairs of buckshee Wild Bunch tickets still on offer after this one from The Deadwood Playboys . . .

The opening chords of 'Lovesick Blues' come crashing in over the airwaves.

Frank [*Opening eyes*] That is all I need . . . [*To Billie*] . . . gonnae turn that off?

Billie turns the volume up.

Frank] Not up . . . off!

Billie [*Over shoulder*] Whereabouts are we headed? You never said.

Frank [*Above song*] I thought Jolene was lookin' up her Yella Pages?

Billie] I cannae hear you.

Frank [*Loudly*] Yella Pages!

Billie] Naw, that was Creedence Clearwater, d'you want to give us a shout when we get there?

Frank] Get where?

Tonto, a short, thickset individual in a baggy suit, enters the Bar-L from the street.

His eyes sweep the banquettes.

Tracey is leaning against the bar waiting for Spencer to prepare a drinks order.

Tonto crosses and perches on the stool next to her.

Tonto [*To Spencer*] Gless a wine, Butch.

He takes a loose cigarette from his top pocket, sticks it in his mouth, and strikes a match against the bar counter.

Tracey] D'you mind?

Tonto pats his jacket pockets.

Tonto] Sorry, darlin', that's ma last wan . . . I'll keep you ma dowt.

Tracey turns away in disgust.

Tonto] Ho, dae us a favour. I'm supposed tae be meetin' somebody only I'm no' too sure if I know whit they luk like . . .

He casts his eyes around.

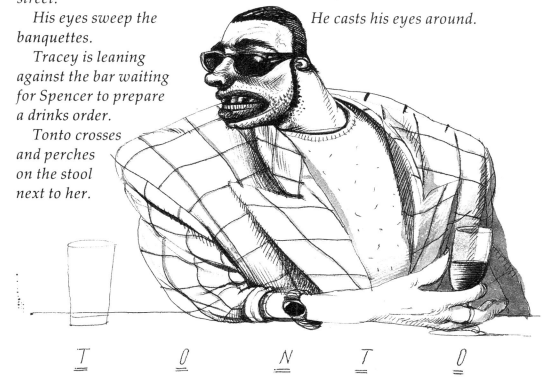

T O N T O

Tracey] I wouldnae worry about it, if they've caught sight of you first, chances are they've legged it awre12dy.

She takes her tray of drinks and moves off.

Tonto] Eh?

Spencer] Red or white?

Tonto] Rid ur white whit?

Spencer] I can let you have a nice Chardonnay at two seventy-five.

Tonto] Naw, jist the wine, Jim . . . in a tumbler . . . fur drinkin', yeh?

Shirley crosses over to the bar.

Shirley] Would you care for a glance at tonight's Specials?

She hands Tonto a menu.

Shirley] There's a Vegetarian Ragout set in a Guacamole Cassis on the back at seven fifty or you might prefer the Crab and Kiwi Junket with continental leaves at six twenty-five?

Tonto] No' got any squerr crisps, naw?

Shirley] Excuse me . . .

Two uniformed police officers enter the bar from the street.
Fraser Boyle emerges from the men's room, wraparound shades in one hand, his other covering his eyes.
He glances up and spots Shirley crossing to speak to the police officers.

Boyle] Oh oh.

He clamps his shades back on and disappears back into the men's room.
As the two police officers cross to the bar, Tonto slides off his stool, slips on his Ray-bans and casually sidles towards the street exit.
As soon as he reaches the street he hurries off towards a dark alleyway by the side of the building.
Tonto enters the alleyway and hastens down it, glancing backwards towards the street.
Just ahead of him a pair of highly-ornamented cowboy boots appear at a small ground floor window.
Suddenly Fraser Boyle drops from the window in front of Tonto who crashes into him.

Boyle] Ho, ya . . .!

Tonto] Sorry, pal, never seen you there . . . you awright?

He checks to see that Boyle is physically intact.

Boyle] Aye, I'm fine, I'm fine . . . chuck pawin' at us.

Boyle draws away and fingers his jacket lapels, turning the collar up.

Tonto] S'long as yur awright . . . nice jaikit . . .

He turns and hurries off.

Boyle dusts himself off and starts walking in the opposite direction, towards the street.

After a few paces he stops.

Boyle [*To himself*] Aw, naw . . .

He pats his hands up and down his jacket, then he slips his hand inside.

Boyle [*Loudly*] Ho, come back here, ya durty vermin!

He turns round and sets off at a gallop along the now deserted alleyway.

Cissie is kneeling in front of her fireplace, her face illuminated by flickering flames.

She has rigged up the Gene Autry wireless to run off the mains and the McPhail Sisters' version of 'These Two Empty Arms' is playing through it. As she listens Cissie is feeding the small blaze in the fireplace with twenty pound notes, of which there is a dwindling pile on the hearthrug.

'The Last Resort' video is running on the TV set at fast forward, again with the sound turned down.

The telephone dangles at end of its cord.

The front doorbell rings, while

Billie and Jolene's voices blend in bitter-sweet harmony.

Cissie continues to feed bank notes on to the flames.

The front doorbell rings again.

Radio DJ [*As record fades*] . . . The McPhail Sisters, Billie and Jolene, disappearing down *The Old Chisholm Trail* with that track from the Radio Kelvin compilation CD, *Country Comes to Calton* . . . Dunky Chisholm with you for the next three and a half hours . . . exactly 10.30 by my trusty Tom Mix timepiece, the latest news headlines from Ward Ferguson . . .

There is a news jingle on the radio.

Radio News Reader] Radio Kelvin News at 10.37 . . .

There is a prolonged knocking at Cissie's front door.

Radio News Reader] . . . Strathclyde Police issued a description tonight of the two men wanted in connection with the brutal murder of . . .

The banging gets heavier.

Radio News Reader] . . . in a City Centre barber shop.

Cissie [*Loudly*] If that's who I think it is, I'm not in!

Radio News Reader] The men . . . one in his early-to-mid thirties, the other with a limp . . . are said to be armed and extremely dangerous . . .

Policeman [*From landing*] Police, open up!

Cissie] Bloody hell . . .

She scoops up the remainder of the bank notes and piles them on to the fire.

Radio News Reader] . . . on a somewhat lighter note, the rooftop protest at a Glasgow jail has now . . .

Cissie reaches across and pulls the plug from the wall socket.

   On the landing outside a policeman and a policewoman are standing with Cissie's elderly neighbour from upstairs.

Policewoman [*Into personal radio*] Naw, still no joy, Chief.

Neighbour] D'you want a hatchet to break the door down?

The policewoman leans down to the letter box.

Policewoman [*Loudly*] If you're in there, love, will you . . .

The door swings open suddenly.

Cissie [*Coldly*] Yes!

Policewoman] Mrs Crouch?

Neighbour] Aye, that's her awright.

Cissie [*To neighbour*] Drop dead, ya old nuisance.

Policewoman] It was just to let you know your husband's fine.

Neighbour] She's had one of her fancy men in there . . . tarted up to the nines . . .

Cissie [*Interrupting. To policewoman*] Fine? What you talkin' about, he's 'fine'?

Tamara MacAskill is standing by the open door of the radio car, talking into the mike.

Tamara [*Into mike*] . . . the prison officer, 48-year-old Mr Donald Ritchie, sustained only minor facial injuries and a fractured pelvis when the 34-year-old rooftop demonstrator landed on top of him in the exercise yard below.

Looking up the prison wall above the radio car it is possible to see a trail of broken slates that marks the trail of Dorwood's downward progress.

Tamara [*Into mike*] Both men are reported to be reasonably comfortable in separate wards of the prison hospital this evening . . .

102

Tamara MacAskill, Radio Kelvin News, Riddrie . . . [*To engineer*] . . . I wonder if the paper managed to get a shot of him coming off the roof . . . d'you want to give them a ring, Brian?

Engineer [*On carphone*] Aye, here she is . . . hold on . . .

He hands the carphone out of the car window.

Engineer [*To Tamara*] . . . sounds like the boyfriend.

Tamara] I don't have a boyfriend, I've got a husband. [*On carphone*] Hi . . . who's this?

Frank [*On phone*] . . . I don't need a hot water bottle or nothin', I'm quite prepared to rough it . . . hullo, Tamara?

Billie is sitting in her parked taxi, radio mike in hand.

Billie [*On radio*] . . . when, there the now, over?

There is a short bark over the radio.

Billie [*On radio*] You might've given us a shout an' I could've switched it on . . . what'd it sound like, over?

There is a long incomprehensible message over the radio.

Frank is still in the phone box, he dials a number and gets the unobtainable tone.
He replaces the receiver, but remains inside the phone box.

Meanwhile Cissie stands at the window of her apartment and watches as a drizzling rain starts to fall.

On the roof of Barlinnie prison a well-thumbed snapshot of a child flutters in the night breeze on the dark slates near a chimney stack.

H   O   B   O

4

Happy Trails

In the slowly lightening morning Billie's taxi is parked outside a scruffy two-storey building, on the ground floor of which is Ronnie's Radio Taxis.

As the wintry sun struggles manfully to clear the rooftops, an elderly hobo shuffles along the icy pavement, dipping every so often to examine some item of interest in the gutter.

There is the faint sound of music in the thin air.

The hobo pauses to rifle a litter bin. A stray cur wanders across the street to sniff at the trail of rubbish in the hobo's wake. As he shuffles abreast of the parked taxi, the hobo sees a discarded Lanliq bottle dully glinting in the feeble rays of the watery sun. He bends to investigate.

The passenger door of the taxi inches open and Frank McClusky's bleary features appear opposite the hobo's at ground level. It is apparent that Frank has spent the night sleeping on the taxi floor. Frank looks at the bottle in the hobo's mitt.

Frank] Naw. I'll stick with my usual, pops . . . pint of Head and Shoulders an' a half-dozen rolls . . .

The rehearsal room above the taxi office is still and bare now, except for a mike stand in the middle of the floor and a 5-watt guitar amp in a battered black case.

Across town, in stark comparison to the quietness of Ronnie's Radio Taxis, an ambulance with a police and prison van escort pulls up at the gates of the huge Victorian Glasgow City Hospital. The vehicles pull off through the gates following signs for the Neurology Unit.

The rehearsal room is now in use again. Jolene idles across to the window as

her fingers wander across the accordion keys.

Jolene [*Over music*] You didnae happen to catch the news on the radio last night, did you?

Billie is concentrating hard on perfecting her fingerwork on a somewhat convoluted guitar riff.

Jolene] Billie?
Billie [*Preoccupied*] What?
Jolene] You didnae happen to catch . . .

Billie abandons her riff.

Billie] Naw . . . an' nor did I happen to catch wur album track's first outing 'cos somebody never thought to get in touch . . .

She carries on strumming while Jolene takes over the melody.

Billie] . . . what you askin' for?
Jolene] Naw, nothin', I was just curious.

Jolene leans forward and peers through the icy window.

Jolene] Yeh, the roofs do look quite slippy . . .
Billie] The what?
Jolene] . . . there's a wee auld guy just fell all his length on to a stray pooch out here.
Billie] On to a which?

Jolene watches the dog struggle out from underneath the hobo, yelping. Frank emerges from the taxi in all the confusion, a pair of cowboy boots in his hand.

Frank [*To stray cur*] Don't let him sit on you, son . . take a bite out his bum . . .

The dog looks at Frank, snarling viciously.

Frank] . . . ahyah, bugger!

He hotfoots it across the pavement in stocking soles and heads for the taxi office as the stray cur rounds on him.
    Upstairs, Jolene and Billie are still talking.

Jolene] Okay, so we've got wurselves a geetar-picker, what about wur chantoose?

They hear the sound of barking and door-slamming from downstairs.

In the waiting room of the City Hospital there is a mixture of visitors and outpatients, all of them silent and sullen.
    A young man, with a shaven head, his face covered in defiant tattoos, chomps on gum, blowing intermittent bubbles and cracking them loudly.

Next to him is an older woman with her husband and two young women. They're all watching Cissie, who paces to and fro in front of them, pulling on a cigarette.

First young woman [*Loudly*] She's smokin'.

Older woman [*To Cissie*] This's supposed to be a hospital.

Second young woman] What aboot hur? She's smokin'.

She accepts a cigarette from her companion, as the older woman's husband takes a packet from his pocket.

Older woman [*To husband*] Get you those away.

Young man] Err she's smokin' . . .

The young man takes a wad of gum from his mouth and hands it to the older woman.

Young man] . . . huv that.

He takes a cigarette from the older woman's husband, breaks the tip off and sticks it in his mouth.

   There is a great plume of smoke as everyone lights up.

Older woman [*Sotto voce, to husband*] Just you wait till I get you home!

Husband [*Between coughs*] Good Christ, wumman, it's the only pleasure I've goat . . .

Tamara MacAskill's head appears round the waiting room door, as the husband has a coughing fit.

Tamara] Is there a Mrs Crouch here?

Older woman] Hell bloody mend you!

Cissie whips round.

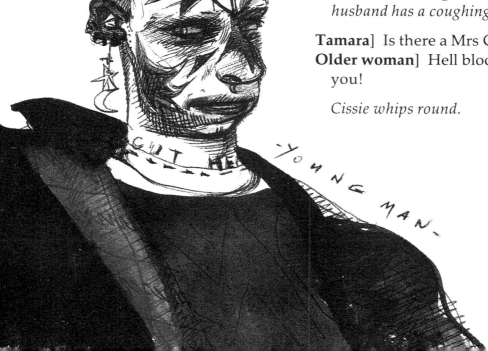

Cissie] How is he?

Tamara] I was just about to ask you the same thing . . .

She enters the room and closes the door quietly behind her.

Tamara] *Evening Echo*, d'you mind having a word? I'm doing a follow-up story on Dorville.

Cissie] Dor-wood.

Tamara] Sorry?

Tamara delves into her bag for a shorthand notebook.

Cissie] Dor-wood!

Cissie starts pacing again, lighting a fresh cigarette from a dogend.

Tamara] I just need a couple of details from you . . .

She flips the shorthand pad open.

Cissie] Yeh, like gettin' his name right . . . slope off.

Tamara] I believe you were quite active on the Western music scene yourself at one time, is that true?

All eyes swivel from Tamara to Cissie.

Cissie] Last night he's fine, this mornin' he's in for a brain scan . . .

All eyes swivel from Cissie to Tamara.

Tamara] How long've you been married?

Cissie] What the hell kind of a jail is it that lets them exercise on the bloody roof in this weather . . .

Tamara] D'you have any kiddies?

Cissie] . . . he's a deep-sea-diver, for God's sake!

Tamara] Did it come as a bit of a shock to you when he got into the lower reaches of the charts earlier this year with . . .

Cissie [*Interrupting*] I wish to God he still was instead of harin' about the country with a bandana round his nut singin' Gene Autry numbers with a bunch of deadbeats an' drug addicts . . .

Tamara] Gene Autry . . . of course . . .

She writes in her notebook.

Cissie] . . . at least I knew where he was when he was trauchlin' about the sea-bed in his . . .

Tamara [*Interrupting*] . . . something about his 'redundancy money'?

Cissie] . . . what'd you say?

She stops dead and looks at Tamara. All eyes swivel to Tamara.

Tamara] Shouted down to the radio car, wanted you to fetch him food and cigarettes . . . of course, Brian and I thought . . .

Cissie] Aw, my God . . .

She sits down with a thump.

Tamara] . . . are you all right? You're as white as a sheet.

Cissie] Naw, I'm fine, I'm fine . . .

A nurse appears at the waiting room door.

Nurse] Is there a Mrs Crouch here?

Frank is seated on the floor of the rehearsal room while Jolene is trying to force a cowboy boot on to one of his feet.

Jolene] It's pretty obvious they've swole up durin' the night . . .

Frank] Don't be ridiculous, if they'd swole up durin' the night I'd be able to get my feet into them this mornin' . . . ohyah . . .

Billie] So who we gonnae phone?

Jolene] What about the wee cobbler's in Maryhill Road?

Frank] Yeh, get him to send over a coupla gallons of thon stretchy paint, this's murder . . .

Billie fixes them with a baleful look.

Billie] To replace the beanpole.

Frank and Jolene [*Together*] Aw . . .

Fraser Boyle presses his finger to the doorbell of Cissie's apartment, and

keeps it there. He has a guitar case in his other hand. The elderly neighbour passes the landing on her way upstairs. She is wearing a slightly scabby fur coat over an overall and slippers and is carrying a half-pint carton of milk.*

Neighbour] Tch, tch, tch, tch, tch, tch . . .

Boyle keeps his finger on the doorbell and watches the woman disappear upstairs.

The apartment door is suddenly thrown open and Cissie appears. She is now dressed in a riding suit with a long divided skirt.

Cissie] I told you awready, I don't want to talk to any report . . .

She breaks off on seeing who it is.

Cissie [*To herself*] . . . aw, God.

Boyle] Thought you werenae in . . .

He places a boot over the doorstep and leans against the doorframe.

Cissie] I've just this minute got back, what d'you want? I'm in a hurry.

She closes the door against Boyle's foot and peers through the remaining gap.

Boyle] I've brung the boy's Dobro.

Cissie] You've what?

Boyle] Brung his Dobro. S'a geetar

wi' a resonator pan in the middle,
d'you no' remember me tellin'
you about it in the . . .

*Cissie reaches out and takes hold of
the guitar case.*

Cissie [*Interrupting*] Yeh, fine, I'll see
that he . . . [*Breaks off*] are you
tryin' to be comical?

Boyle] Naw, too quick,
Gorgeous . . . that's
what you say after I've
asked you.

Cissie] Asked me what?

Boyle] If you can lend me some
dough?

Cissie] Are you tryin' to be comical?

Boyle] See? That's what all your best
double acts've got . . .

Cissie] You know he fell
off the roof, don't you?

Boyle [*Interrupting*] . . . timin'.
What?

Cissie] Dorwood . . . he fell off the
roof last night . . . it was on the
news.

Boyle] You're kiddin' . . .

He looks up the stairwell.

Cissie] Not this roof . . . D-Wing,
he's in intensive care, I've just
come back to get his rosary beads!

Boyle] That bad? Jesus . . . look, I'll
let you have it back, Friday . . .

Cissie] Let me have what back
Friday?

*The elderly neighbour reappears from
upstairs and passes across the
landing.*

Neighbour] Tch, tch, tch, tch, tch,
tch . . .

110

Cissie [*Loudly*] He's only bringin' Dorwood's Dobro back!

Boyle [*Loudly*] I'm only bringin' the boy's Dobro back . . . [*To Cissie*] . . . d'you want me to run after the auld bag an' give her a kickin'?

Cissie] Beat it, ya louse.

She tries closing the door but the guitar case gets in the way.

Boyle] Heh, c'mon, sweetheart, I'm tryin' to be nice to you while ma best buddy's in the jile, yeh?

He leans a hand against the door panel.

Cissie] The only time you ever try to be 'nice' is when you're after somethin', an' right now your best buddy' isn't in the jail, he's in a locked ward at the City Hospital with a suspected cerebral haemorrhage!

Boyle] What's that – nose bleeds, yeh?

Cissie] If he dies you've had it . . .

Boyle] Dies?

Cissie] You've had it, anyhow . . . now, get!

She tries forcing the door shut.

Boyle] I wouldnae do that, Gorgeous . . . if there's one thing that drives me nuts it's . . .

Cissie] Bugger off!

Boyle] . . . awright, awright, you're upset, I can see that . . tell you what I'll do . . . save you gettin' this door rehung . . . I'll come inside an' you an' I'll discuss how much you want to give us over a cuppa coffee, how's that?

He forces the door open and shoves his way past Cissie into the flat.

Cissie] Hoi, come back here, where the hell d'you think you're goin'?

Frank, one boot half-on, hirples towards the door of the rehearsal room.

Frank [*To Billie*] I'm only goin' to wash my gizzard . . .

Billie] Don't you do a runner, d'you hear?

Frank pauses at the door, gives a quick glance down, looks across at Billie, then exits.

Jolene [*Shouts from downstairs*] You there, Billie?

Billie consults her song-list on the floor in front and carries on working out chords on the guitar.

Frank] [*Shouts from outside door*] What one's the toilet?

Jolene [*Shouts from downstairs*] Billie?

Billie [*Loudly*] How's wee Desmond fixed, can he do it?

Jolene [*Still shouting*] I wasnae

111

phonin' wee Desmond. I was phonin' the boy MacIndoo . . .

Billie [*Loudly*] Can the boy MacIndoo do it?

Jolene [*Shouting, but tailing off*] I'm just about to phone wee Desmond.

Frank finds the drivers' toilet. It is a very basic affair with peeling walls and graffiti-covered doors. He opens one of the cubicle doors and looks inside. He frowns.

Frank] Well, one thing's for sure . . . I'm certainly not doin' an Elvis down that one . . .

Cissie's Gene Autry radio is on, 'Don't be Cruel' blaring from it.

Boyle [*Sings along*] ' . . . if you don't come around, at least, please telephone . . .'

In the kitchen Cissie removes a coffee mug from the oven, with the aid of a dish towel, and places it on a tray.

Boyle [*Still singing*] ' . . . don't be cruel, to a heart that's true . . .'

Boyle is perched on the arm of a chair, with the radio on his lap.

Boyle [*Singing*] ' . . . don't want no other love . . . baby, it's still you . . .'

He breaks off as Cissie enters with the red-hot mug on a tray.

Boyle] . . . I remember the night me an' Dorwood bought this off the boy up in Oilsville . . .

Cissie] Here . . . grab that.

Boyle lays the radio aside and takes hold of the mug handle in his gloved hand.

Boyle] . . . cheeky sod wanted two hunner bucks for it . . .

He raises the scalding mug to within a half-inch of his lips.

Boyle] . . . I goes like thon.

He lowers the mug and gives his 'radio seller' look.

Boyle] He goes like that. I goes . . .

He raises the scalding mug to his lips again?

Boyle] So, tell me, how's the boy?

He lowers the mug without its having touched his lips.

Cissie] On the critical list.

Boyle:] Not that 'boy', the boy, yeh?

Boyle raises the scalding mug to his lips and is just about to drink . . .

Boyle] I don't see his pitcher up . . .

He lowers the mug and looks around

the bare walls.

Boyle] . . . in fact, I don't see any pitchers up . . . this you doin' a moonlight?

He gets up and crosses to some packing cases, mug in hand.

Cissie] Come outta there.

Boyle] I remember you used to have a big coloured-in snapshot of him in thon cowboy gear I bought for his Christmas.

Boyle pokes around the tea-chests.

Cissie] What cowboy gear? You bought him a baseball cap an' a pair of Johnny Sheffield swimmin' trunks that nearly drowned him . . .

Cissie gets up and goes over to Boyle and stuffs some crumpled notes into his top pocket.

Cissie] . . . there's twenty-seven quid there, drink up an' disappear.

Boyle lays aside the scalding mug without having set a lip to it and reaches for the crumpled notes in his top pocket.

Boyle] They werenae Johnny Sheffield swimmin' trunks, they were Johnny Mack Brown junior competition chaps, he would've grew into them . . .

He smooths the crumpled notes out.

Boyle] . . . you no' heard nothin', naw? Must be comin' up for startin' school . . . what's that, about a year?

Cissie] Seven months. When're you leavin' so I can fumigate the place.

Boyle] Seven months? No' long in goin' in, eh? Any luck an' he'll've forgot all about you . . . 'much did you say was here?

Cissie] What d'you need it for? Thought you were makin' plenty off that fish . . . don't sit there countin' it!

Boyle [*Interrupting*] . . . twenty-two, twenty-three, twenty-four . . . I make it twenty-five. Twenty-five quid isnae gonnae purchase what I'm after . . . naw, hold on, there's two stuck tegither . . . lemme start again . . . one . . . two . . . three . . . four . . .

Cissie] Are you goin' to leave right now or do I have to get on that phone?

Boyle] Who are you gonna phone, your Probation Officer?

He laughs.

Boyle] Seven, eight, nine . . .

Cissie] I mean it!

Boyle] . . . eleven, twelve, thirteen . . . what'd you get him for his burthday? November, innit? Or did you forget? Naw, naw, that's perfectly understandable . . . takes a good coupla years for the old brain cells to knit back into place after takin' that kind of a doin' . . . fourteen, fifteen . . . you still go to the meetin's, yeh? Sixteen, seventeen . . .

Cissie] I'm warnin' you . . .

Lena Martell's 'One Day at a Time' is playing low on the radio.

Boyle] . . . ho, there's your theme tune.

He reaches out and turns the volume up.

Boyle [*Sings along*] ' . . . show me the way, one day at a time . . .'

Cissie] Get that off.

Boyle] S'up . . . no' makin' you thursty, is it?

Cissie] Get it off, I said!

She makes a breenge for the radio, but Boyle grabs a hold of her, laughing. Cissie attacks him with her fists.

Boyle] Ho, chuck that!

He grabs Cissie by the wrists.

Cissie [*Enraged*] Aaaaargh . . .

Boyle] S'no' ma fault he got took into care . . .

Cissie] . . . I'm gonnae kill you!

Boyle] Aye, like hell you are . . . it's a

blue do when a peace-lovin' guy cannae check up on his kid's welfare without some crazy doll . . .

Cissie [*Interrupting*] Who said he was yours!

Boyle] C'mon, Gorgeous, you werenae that drunk you cannae recall all they times when Dorwood was splashin' about in the deeps an' you an' me were . . .

He pulls Cissie close.

Cissie] You an' me were what! Quit maulin' us . . .

She struggles to get free.

Boyle] . . . used to be right friendly, us guys . . . d'you no' remember?

He starts kissing Cissie's neck.

Cissie] You're forgettin', I'm an amnesiac . . . gerroffa me . . .

Boyle] Lemme remind you . . .

He kisses her throat.

Cissie] . . . chuck that. [*Softening*] Chuck it, I said . . . naw, please, Fraser, don't . . . pl . . .

Boyle's mouth is on hers.
Cissie continues to struggle during the long embrace but her struggles grow less until she melts.

Boyle [*Coming up for air*] . . . d'you remember now?

Cissie reaches down and unbuckles Boyle's belt. She unzips his jeans. Boyle's eyes roll, and shut.

Boyle [*Hoarsely*] She remembers . . . aw, God . . .

Cissie [*Huskily*] D'you mind if I . . . ?

Boyle [*Quickly*] . . . naw, naw . . . do it, do it . . .

Cissie] You sure you want me to?

Boyle [*Eyes shut*] . . . sure I'm sure, just hurry up an' . . .

Boyle's eyes burst open in horror.

Boyle] . . .waaaaaaaaaaaaaaaaaaaagh!

Boyle clutches at his scalded crotch with both hands.

Cissie] One for the souvenir album, right!

Boyle] Ya bitch!

Cissie chucks the now empty coffee mug at him, grabs the Dobro case and makes a beeline for the front door.

Outside the Bar-L Tracey is fixing a hand-printed notice to the front door. It reads: 'WE ARE CLOSED. NEAREST SOUL FOOD BAR "THE DIXIECUP", 418 W12 St, NYC.' Tracey goes back inside and crosses to the banquette where Shirley sits, in her street clothes, with the early edition of the Evening Echo. *There is a head and shoulders picture of David Cole on the front page of the paper under a big headline which reads, 'Barber Shop Slaughter', with a smaller picture of barber Eric next to a sub-heading of 'Close Shave for Eric'.*

Tracey] What'd Detroit say when you phoned? D'you tell them he got murdered?

Shirley] They never said nothin' . . . just to pay off the kitchen staff, lock everythin' up, an' somebody from some lawyer's office, I didnae quite catch, would be along to pick up the keys . . . that could be anytime. What'm I supposed to do, sit about here an' wait to get my head blown off?

Tracey] That's what you get the extra one seventy-five a week for, Shirley. I'll get you a coffee.

Tracey crosses to the bar.

Shirley] What d'you reckon it is, some kinda vendetta? There's that Italian guy with the hair round the corner . . .

Tracey] The fishburger franchise?

Shirley] . . . he also does filled rolls. You don't know what gets into some people . . . I'm just readin' in here about a lassie that got both her ears bitten off at a dance in the City Chambers an' she's not even heard from the Polis . . . don't gimme any sugar, I want to get into they cream culottes I got for Wee Sandra's twenty-first on Thursday.

She flicks over another page in the newspaper.

Shirley] Aw, my God . . . hey, Tracey, look at this, who's that?

She holds the newspaper up to show a picture of Dorwood, his head bandaged so that only the eyes show, under a headline which reads: 'SLIPPERY CUSTOMER FOR HIGH JUMP SAY DOCS'.

Tracey] The Invisible Man?
Shirley] Naw, it's him . . . big thingmy's husband . . . accordin' to this he's at death's door.

Dorwood lies on a bed in his hospital room. Only his eyes show in his bandaged head, and they are shut.
*   There is a knock at the closed door. The prison officer at Dorwood's bedside folds his newspaper, gets up, and crosses to unlock the door. The prison chaplain enters and walks across to the bed. He lays out his last rites paraphernalia.*

In another part of town Cissie is trudging through the freezing streets with Dorwood's Dobro. She eventually finds a phone box, dumps the Dobro on the ground, and searches through her pockets for some money.

In Ronnie's Radio Taxis' office Jolene sits straddled on a chair with her chin resting on her hands. She's chomping on some gum. Billie stands in the entrance holding the door open.

Billie [*Loudly*] Are you gonnae get a move on up there! [*To Jolene*] Have you phoned to cancel yet?
Jolene] I'm waitin' to hear back from wee Desmond . . .
Billie] I thought you spoke to him awready an' he couldnae do it?
Jolene] I'm just after buyin' myself a new rigout.
Billie] What kinda answer's that? Are you gonnae hurry up!

The telephone on the table rings.

Jolene] I told him to get his mother to call . . . [*On phone*] Ronnie's Radio Cabs, s'that you, Mrs Devaney?

Frank comes clomping down the stairs, one boot on, the other still only half-on.

Frank] You don't happen to have a very long shoehorn, by any chance?

Billie] Out.

She jerks a thumb towards the street.

Jolene [*On phone*] Hold on . . . [*To Billie*] Will we accept a transfer-charge call from a Glasgow telephone box?

Frank] Or a half pound of margarine might do the trick . . .

Billie [*To Jolene*] Is it for a taxi?

Frank] Naw, it's for this stupit boot . . .

Jolene [*On phone*] Is it a taxi they're after?

Billie [*To Frank*] Right, you . . . adios.

Jolene [*To Billie*] Who d'we know cried . . . [*On phone*] what was their name again?

The prison chaplain anoints Dorwood's bandaged forehead. Dorwood lies still in his bed.

Chaplain] Through this holy anointing may the Lord in his love and mercy help you with the grace of the Holy Spirit.

Prison Officer] Amen.

Chaplain] Lord Jesus Christ, our Redeemer, cure the weakness of your servant, Dorwood . . . heal his sickness and forgive his sins. Expel all afflictions of mind and body, mercifully restore him to . . .

There is a deep sigh from Dorwood and the prison chaplain leans his head down towards the bed.

Chaplain [*With renewed urgency*] . . . may you live in peace this day, may your home be with God in Zion, with Mary, the virgin Mother of God, with Joseph and all the angels and saints.

He makes the sign of the cross over Dorwood.

Prison Officer] Amen.

Fraser Boyle comes hobbling painfully into the living-room of Cissie's apartment, sticking a wet flannel down the front of his jeans. He hobbles across to the phone and picks up the receiver. He rattles the rest up and down and listens. He takes the receiver away from his ear and glares at it.

Boyle] Ya bitch . . .

He picks up the handset, rips its cord from the wall, and smashes the lot into the fireplace.

He takes a swing at the TV and boots the screen in.

Boyle] . . . bitch!

Billie's guitar is propped up against the wall of the taxi office, Jolene's accordion sits on the table. The phone is off the hook.

Jolene, with a large pair of shears in her hand, is concentrating on cutting up two sets of old street maps, selecting the least tatty sections from each, and sellotaping the pieces together into one large, if slightly misleading, entity.

Jolene] You never mentioned what outfits you played with . . .

Frank sits on the stairs, still struggling in vain to get the remaining boot on.

Frank] Naw?
Jolene] We asked you several times but you kept goin' to the toilet.
Frank] It was that brown lentil lasagne Shorty made for supper last night . . . if there's one thing . . .
Jolene [*Interrupting*] That was Boston Bean Broulé an' it was me that made it . . .

Frank [*Quickly*] Naw, naw, it was very . . . what could you say? unusual . . . I might even write a piece about it . . . in fact, I saved some on my shurt so I could send it away an' have it analysed . . . look.

He displays a stain on his shirt front.

Jolene] You're askin' for a fat lip.
Frank] Am I?
Jolene] Chuck tryin' to be smart, I've had better patter offa bumper sticker. Were they mostly all Country, yeh?

Frank has returned to his ongoing struggle with the recalcitrant boot.

Frank] Were what mostly all . . .?
Jolene] Your outfits?
Frank] Naw, this's just camouflage . . . I tend towards a Harris tweed two-piece an' a brogue pump, myself . . . aw, sorry . . . bands we talkin' about? Country-ish, yeh . . . you ever come across The Texas Chainsaw Trio? They had a bazooka in their lineup . . .
Jolene] A bazooki, you mean?
Frank] Naw, a bazooka . . . they were heavily into martial rock at the start . . . blew a big hole in the boy Henderson's good cardigan at one of the university hops, his Maw had a leary . . . that's when we

swapped over to 'swamp music' . . . lead singer was the spittin' double of Jerry Reid . . .

He tugs at his boot.

Frank] . . . or was it Al Reid? I'm not too sure . . . you wouldnae like to give us hand with this, would you?

Jolene] Here . . . why don't you just cut the legs off an' have them as slip-ons?

Jolene holds out her shears.

Frank] That's an idea.

He goes to take the shears, but Jolene snatches them away.

Jolene] God, you would, as well . . . there must be four hunner bucks' worth of boot there . . .

Frank] You reckon?

Jolene] . . . more like seven or eight hunner . . . I used to go out with a guy an' he had a pair that were identical, only newer.

Frank] They don't come any newer . . . any newer an' they're still chewin' the cud.

Jolene] He only ever wore them the once.

Frank] I'm not surprised.

Jolene] Took us to this pancake roadhouse in Faifley when I passed my drivin' test . . . you ever been there?

Frank] Only the once.

Jolene] I'm not surprised . . . you couldnae tell what was the pancake an' what was the plate, they were identical.

Frank] Mebbe you're meant to gnaw them, naw?

Jolene] We tried that, you still couldnae tell.

Frank] Naw, the boots . . . mebbe you're meant to gnaw them?

Jolene] Gnaw them?

Frank] Yeh, gnaw. Here . . . d'you fancy gnawin' that for us?

He holds the boot out to Jolene.

Frank] S'what your Eskimo does with his footwear of a mornin' . . . gets his old lady to gnaw it for him . . .

Jolene [*Ignoring boot*] So what's with you an' the beanpole?

Frank] . . . softens them up a treat . . .

Jolene] Last time me an' Billie bumped into her was ten years back . . .

Frank] . . . feart yur fillin's'll fall out, yeh?

Jolene] . . . where's she been hidin' all this time?

Frank] S'far as I know she hasnae been hidin' . . .

Jolene] Good friend of mine said she seen her up in Aberdeen last Christmas with a toddler in a go-chair . . . you an' her winchin', yeh?

Frank] Naw . . . an' chuck referrin' to her as 'the beanpole', her right name's Cissie.

Jolene] What's that short for . . . Cystitis?

Frank] Now you're askin' for a fat lip.

Jolene] Aw, yeh? Like who's gonnae gimme one . . . you?

Frank] Could be.

Jolene] Away you go, you couldnae hang a fat lip on a Hallow'en cake if I gave you a pipin' bag fulla marzipan.

Boyle is in a phone box in the street near Cissie's apartment

Boyle [*On phone*] . . . naw . . . 'Winnie', like in 'Pooh', an' 'bay-go', as in 'bay-go' . . . 'Winnie . . . bay-go' . . . what? Naw, that's the make of trailer they're in, the party's name is Jim Bob O'May . . . naw . . . Bob, capital O, apostrophe, M-a-y, as in 'Darling Buds Of . . .', they've got one of these portaphones, you must've number . . . he's no' got an address, that's what I'm sayin' . . . I've just looked, they're no' there . . . what d'you suppose I'm phonin' Directory Enquiries for? They've moved . . . what? 'Cos they got fed up gettin' parkin' tickets, how the hell should I . . . hullo?

He takes the receiver away from his ear and stares at it.

Boyle] Ya cheeky . . . !

Cissie has now arrived at the rehearsal room and sits with Frank in one corner while Billie and Jolene sit in the other. Billie is tuning her guitar while Jolene straps her accordion on. Cissie bends down to the guitar case on the floor, and springs the catches.

Frank] Boy, am I glad to see you, they were all for givin' us the heave an' gettin' wee MacIndoo an' boy Desmond in . . . what'd you say this was . . . a Dumbo?

Cissie] Dobro . . . Dopyera Brothers, 1932 . . . it's got a resonator pan in the middle . . .

Frank] Ah, yeh, right . . . [*To Billie and Jolene*] S'got a resonator pan in the middle . . .

Cissie] Dorwood only ever played it the once so watch it . . .

She lifts the Dobro out of its case.

Frank] C'mon, you're talkin' to the guy that inherited a Skiffle-jo . . .

Cissie] How's the arm?

Frank takes the guitar from her.

Frank] Naw, that's the neck . . . looks awright to me, s'not warped or nothin' . . .

He runs a thumb across the strings.

Cissie] That arm.

She gives Frank's tattoo a prod.

Frank] Ohyah . . . sore . . . kept me up all night . . .

He slips the Dobro around his neck.

Frank] . . . that an' the brown lentil lasagne . . . so, what made you change your mind? Not that I'm not grateful. I thought I was never gonnae see you again . . . wasnae anythin' to do with . . .

He footers with the tuning pegs.

Frank] . . . your discoverin' somethin'?

Cissie] Yeh, I discovered where that eighteen grand came from . . .
Frank] Naw, I meant somethin' to do with you an' me . . .
Cissie [*Interrupting*] . . . an' how much I loathe that crummy slug.
Frank] . . . okay, so it's a banal scenario . . . boy meets girl . . boy falls head over heels . . . boy gets head punched in . . . boy gets tattoo . . .

Cissie] Give us a coupla quid, will you?
Frank] . . . boy parts with all his dosh . . .

Frank produces a single one pound note.

Cissie] That's just eighteen fifty you owe me.

She pockets the pound note.

Frank] . . . tell me about this toddler.
Cissie [*Sharply*] What toddler?
Billie] You ready, you pair?

She and Jolene make their way to the mike.

Frank] I'm ready . . . what d'you want to kick off with . . . 'Billy Goat Gruff'?

Billie and Jolene freeze in their tracks.

Frank] It's about the only cowboy number I know all the verses to . . .

Fraser Boyle's fish van lurches to a halt outside Timberwolf Tierney's (aka The Tall Cowpoke's) DIY store in Cowcaddens.

Boyle climbs gingerly out, a lumpy newspaper-wrapped parcel under his arm. He hobbles painfully across the pavement.

DREW &
ROXANNE

Inside the store Roxanne is serving a customer.

Roxanne] Is it furra boudoir? [*Loudly*] We goat any they 'easy-assemble' wardrops in stock? Thur's a customer oot here luckin' fur a tallboy. [*To customer*] Jist the wan, aye?

Boyle shoves the door open and hobbles in.

Roxanne [*Loudly*] Jist the wan. [*Greeting Boyle*] Well, howdy, stranger . . . huvnae saw you since the hot-dog stall at the Cowdenbeath Rodeo . . . this you hud yur vasectomy? [*Loudly*] Ye there, Timber?

In the backshop Drew and the Tall Cowpoke are sitting with their feet up enjoying a late lunch.
  Drew is poring over a crossword on the 'Fun Page' of the early edition of the Evening Echo.

Drew [*Reads*] 'Seven across . . . "Asbestos underpants no answer to Jerry Lee's outsize spherical blazers?" . . . five, five, two, an' four . . .'

Boyle hobbles through into the backshop clutching his parcel.

Drew [*Musing*] . . . 'Asbestos underpants no answer to . . .'

Tall Cowpoke [*To Boyle*] Ye want some coffee? Still hoat . . .

He pours himself a cup.
  Boyle dumps the parcel on the table and unwraps it.

Drew [*Musing*] ' . . . Outsize spherical blazers?'
Boyle] 'Much?'

The Tall Cowpoke eyes Cissie's Gene Autry radio.

Tall Cowpoke] Whit is it, a cigarette boax?

Boyle plugs the radio into a socket.

Drew [*Musing*] ' . . . Asbestos underpants?'

The radio stutters into life playing the Wild Bunch Fiddlers' version of Jerry Lee's 'Great Balls of Fire'.

Tall Cowpoke] Aah . . . s'a musical cigarette boax . . .
Boyle] S'a Gene Autry wireless, ya mug.

Boyle switches the radio off as Roxanne enters the backshop.

Roxanne] D'ye no' hear me shoutin'?

The Tall Cowpoke examines the radio.

Tall Cowpoke] Where d'ye pit the fags, in the back?

Roxanne [*To Drew*] Away oot an' ask that customer is it aw wan if it's a 'vanitry' unit? I cannae see any wardrops . . .

Tall Cowpoke [*To Boyle*] Tenner suit ye?

He pulls a wad of bills, receipts, banknotes, and invoices from his dungaree pockets.

Boyle] That's worth at least a hunner, ya doughball . . . if she hadnae took the Dobro I wouldnae've came here.

Roxanne [*To Drew*] They come in rid, off-white, an' olive, tell him.

Drew chucks his newspaper aside and slouches out to the frontshop, stuffing a fried egg roll into his face.

Boyle] Make it fifteen.

Tall Cowpoke] I huvnae goat fifteen . . .

Roxanne [*Loudly, to Drew*] Thur's wan olive left . . .

The Tall Cowpoke sifts through the litter from his pockets.

Tall Cowpoke] . . . two fives . . . three wans . . . four two bob bits . . .

Roxanne [*Loudly to Drew*] . . . naw I tell a lie, it's avacadda . . .

Tall Cowpoke] . . . an' them's yur invoices.

Boyle] What invoices?

Tall Cowpoke] I'm gonnae huv a joab gettin' squerred up offa cadaiver, umn't I?

Boyle runs an eye down the invoices.

Boyle [*Reads*] 'Seventeen hinges . . . five pund of screwnails . . .'?

Tall Cowpoke] D'ye want tae dae a cheque?

He slides Drew's ballpoint pen across the table to Boyle.

Boyle] I've awready done a check . . . last night . . . couldnae believe ma . . . 'cadaiver', what 'cadaiver'?

Tall Cowpoke] Yankee boy . . . goat hissel' offed at the herrdresser's . . .

He picks up the Echo *and folds it to the front page.*

Boyle] Got hissel' what?

Roxanne [*Loudly, to Drew*] . . . unless he wants tae go fur the beej, which I personally think luks clatty.

Boyle snatches the paper from the Tall Cowpoke's hand.

Boyle] . . . Holy Christ.

Shirley is seated at one of the Bar-L banquettes, a plug-in phone to her ear, and a pen poised over the 'Sits Vac' page of the Evening Echo. *A long list of vacancies have been*

scored through in felt-tip.

Shirley [*On phone*] . . . yeh, I've eaten there myself, I must say it was very nice . . . would you like me to bring along my diploma from Hamburger University?

There is a rattle at the Bar-L front door.

Shirley [*On phone*] No, this was the three-day residential course in microwave technology and personal hygiene . . .

The front door rattles again.

Shirley [*On phone*] . . . no, hygiene . . .

The rattle gets more insistent.

Shirley [*On phone*] . . . sure, no problem . . . see you then, then . . . thanks, bye.

She replaces the receiver and circles the Pancake Roadhouse vacancy.
The front door rattles violently.

Shirley [*Loudly*] Yeh, awright, I'm comin'.

She gathers up a bunch of keys. She sees a shadowy figure fuzzily visible on the other side of frosted-glass deco door. She sticks the key in the lock, makes a half-turn, and hesitates.

Shirley [*To herself*] Yeh, that's right,

get your stupit head blown off. [*Aloud*] We're shut. Who is it?

Inside the taxi office Billie stands by the front door, straining her eyes in the gathering dusk. Frank and Jolene sprawl in their chairs.

Frank] . . . Doris Day, your bahookey.

Jolene] It was so Doris Day . . . [*To Billie*] Who sang 'Windy City' on the *Perry Como Hogmanay Special* in 1958?

Billie [*Looking out of the door*] If she's not off this next bus that's it . . .

Frank [*To Jolene*] D'you give in?

Jolene] If this's another one of your trick questions you're gettin' that boot rammed down your gullet . . .

Billie [*Turning*] I don't know if you realise, Jolene, but we're in serious trouble here . . .

Jolene] Naw, we're not, we'll catch up . . . [*To Frank*] Right, this's for twenty points . . . what famous Country singer . . .

Frank [*Interrupting*] You havenae answered the previous question . . .

Billie [*Interrupting*] I'm not talkin' about your stupit game! I'm talkin' about the beanpole!

Frank] Chuck callin' her that, I've

125

awready chastised her for . . .

Billie] Shuttup!

Billie paces the length of the room and stands with her hands against the wall, looking at the floor.

Jolene [*Sotto voce, to Frank*] What famous Country singer appeared in the John Ford movie, *My Darling Clem . . .*'

Frank [*Interrupting*] Roy Acuff!

Billie] Shuttup, I said!

Ralph Henderson, of Melon, Brolly and Henderson, solicitors, stands inside the Bar-L Piano Bar and Grill and casts his eyes upwards to the art deco detail around him.

Shirley] . . . Tracey an' I's wiped the surfaces an' turfed all the perishables out the back for the bin motor, Mr . . . ?

Shirley, dressed for going home, pulls on her gloves.

Shirley] . . . sorry, I didn't catch your name through the glass.

Henderson] Henderson . . . Ralph [*Pronouncing it 'Raif'*], Melon, Brolly and Henderson . . . Jamaica Street.

He passes a business-card to Shirley.

Henderson] Tell me something . . .

Shirley] . . . Shirley.

Henderson] . . . is that a pokey hat?

Shirley's hand instinctively goes to her head.

Shirley] Naw, it's a beret.

Henderson] No . . . up there.

Shirley] Where?

She follows Henderson's gaze upwards.

Shirley] Aw, yeh . . . so it is.

She and Henderson ponder the frieze for some moments.

Henderson] Don't let me keep you.

Shirley] Naw, right. If you ever find yourself footloose in Faifley an' feel like a pancake, give us a phone . . .

She moves towards the door.

Shirley] . . . I've left wur uniforms folded inside the Blüthner . . . bye.

She goes out into the street.
Moments later Tonto enters the bar.

Tonto] Thought that gabby doll wis never gonnae go . . . where d'you want us to start?

*In a corridor of the Glasgow City
Hospital Cissie is standing in front of
a grim-faced nurse.*

Cissie] What d'you mean I'm too
late? I'd to come on the bus, I've
brought his bedsocks an' his rosary
beads . . .

       Nurse] I really am awful
sorry, Mrs Crouch.

      *Cissie pushes a hospital
room door open and
stares at an empty bed, its sheets
thrown back.*

Cissie] Sorry? What you tellin' me
sorry!

*Jim Bob's Winnebago is parked in the
darkness outside the Ponderosa club
in Wishaw.*

   *Jim Bob and his band The Wild
Bunch are onstage inside the club for
a soundcheck.*

   *Jim himself is in a crumpled linen
suit. He leans into his mike and
delivers the words of Hank Williams'
lament 'Your Cheatin' Heart' with
an off-handed conviction.*

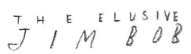

THE ELUSIVE
JIM BOB

Billie is driving the taxi on the road to Wishaw. Frank and Jolene are crammed into the back seat with all sorts of clothing and equipment.

Billie] . . . Naw, *you're* gonnae have to explain.

Frank] Me? Why me?

Billie [*Over shoulder*] 'Cos it was you that got us into this mess!

Frank] S'not my fault she vanished off the face of the earth.

Billie] It was you that gave her the quid!

Jolene] I told you we shoulda hung on till Mrs Devaney phoned.

Billie] What time we supposed to be on at?

Jolene] Lemme find out . . . pull over here.

The taxi pulls up at the corner where a newsvendor has his pitch.

Newsvendor [*Hoarsely*] Err's yur *Times, Echo*, feeeeenell!

Jolene leans her head out of the cab window and whistles.
   The newsvendor flips an Echo *out of the bundle under his arm and crosses to the taxi.*

Newsvendor] Err's yur thirty-five pee, sweetheart.

He holds out the folded copy of the Echo.

Jolene] I thought it was only twenty?

Newsvendor] Err's yur fifteen pence delivery charge, darlin'.

Jolene] Err's yur fifty, get yourself some elocution lessons.

The taxi pulls away from the kerb.
   Jolene flicks through the pages of the Echo.

Frank] Hey, is that not . . . ?

He gestures at a picture on the front page.

Billie [*Over shoulder*] You found it?

Jolene] Gimme a tick, I'm still . . .

She carries on flicking the pages.

Jolene [*To herself*] . . . aargh!

Frank bends his head to get another view of the front page. He sees David Cole's picture.

Frank] Mebbe it's just me but this guy on the front page . . .

Jolene suddenly rips out the page with Dorwood's 'Invisible Man' picture and scrunches it into a ball. Underneath are the entertainment listings.

Jolene] . . . quarter past.

She chucks the scrunched-up paper ball into the space between the front seats.

Billie [*Over shoulder*] Quarter past what? It's nearly ten to the now . . .

Frank eases the scrunched-up paper ball towards his hand, and picks it up. He surreptitiously un-scrunches it.

Jolene] Aw, naw . . .
Billie] What?
Jolene] . . . naw, it's awright, I thought I'd left my new rigout back at the ranch . . .

Frank steals a sideways squint at the torn-out page with Dorwood's picture on it.

Jolene] . . . I got the fright of my life there.

Frank mouths the report on Dorwood's 'Fight for Life' in astonishment . . . until it is snatched from his grasp by Jolene.
  He looks at her as she scrunches the page up into a ball again and stuffs it in the ashtray.

A straggle of cowboys and cowgirls make their way towards the dimly-lit entrance to the Ponderosa Club.

The Tall Cowpoke's 'covered wagon' pulls up alongside the Winnebago, and the Tall Cowpoke, Drew, and Roxanne disembark.

Cissie stands thumbing a lift along the darkened Wishaw road. A snatch of Jim Bob O'May's version of 'Your Cheatin' Heart' hits her ears as a van drives past. She breaks into a run as the van's brakelights flash on some twenty yards up the road.
  Cissie reaches the van, slides the door open and clambers gratefully aboard. 'Your Cheatin' Heart' is still on the radio.

Cissie] You're not goin' anywhere near . . .

Fraser Boyle leans across Cissie and locks the van door.

Boyle] 'Course I'm are . . .
Cissie] Aaaargh . . .

Meanwhile, in the back of the van, two eyes glint through slits in bandages behind the fish crates in the darkened interior as they lurch towards Wishaw.

HAIR STYLIST

5

Lay That Pistol Down, Babe

MONDAY/TUESDAY

Ralph Henderson, divested of his camel coat and suit jacket, is standing up to his armpits in a sinkful of polythene-wrapped frozen, partly-frozen, defrosting and defrosted lobsters in the kitchen of the Bar-L. The kitchen itself is in chaos, as if someone has been searching unsuccessfully for something.

Henderson chucks yet another red herring into the sink.

There is a series of crashes and splinterings from elsewhere in the building.

Henderson wipes his hands on his trouser seat and crosses to the kitchen door. He walks into the dim and deserted bar.

Tonto limps in from the men's room.

Tonto] Nothin' in the toilets either . . .

Tonto chucks a length of splintered doorframe on to the floor.

Henderson] Have you searched his office?

Tonto] Ripped it apart . . . came across a perra slingbacks an' a Billy Daniels LP . . . apart fae that . . . zilch.

Henderson] It's got to be here somewhere . . .

Henderson] . . . you can't lose ten kilos that easily in a joint this size!

Up on top of the building above their heads, nestling inside the giant glowing Ragazzo's half-round 'pokey hat' cornet shell, is a brown paper-wrapped polythene bag of pure Bolivian cocaine, tipping the scales at something just under 18 lbs.

★ ★ ★

Up the road at Wishaw, Jim Bob's Winnebago gleams bulbously in the moonlight outside the Ponderosa Club.

Just inside the door of the club Frank is clutching the receiver of a pay-phone to his ear.

Frank [*On phone*] . . . Sorry Trish, I'm having to shout . . .

Onstage Jim Bob O'May is belting out a lively version of 'Jambalaya'.

Frank [*On phone*] . . . there's a buncha Hibernian ho-downers hollerin' into my left earlobe, I'm just phonin' to check if you got my Peking Duck copy?

Frank is clutching a copy of the Evening Echo *in his other hand.*

Frank [*On phone*] . . . naw . . . 'Duck', Trish . . . 'king' as in 'Cole', 'Duck' as in 'David' . . .

He casts an eye down Tamara MacAskill's front page account of David Cole's murder.

Frank [*On phone*] . . . correction . . . 'Donald' . . . sorry, say again?

He hears a continuous beep-beep as the pay-phone runs out of money. Frank wedges the phone against his ear, Echo *between his teeth, and delves both hands into his Burberry pockets. He stuffs a ten pence piece into the slot and plucks the newspaper from his mouth, leaving a large chunk of front page adhering to his bottom lip.*

Frank [*On phone*] . . . naw, as in 'hoi polloi' . . . it's an oriental . . .

[*spits*] . . . oriental ketchup, you spread it on your . . . [*spits*] . . . naw, your pancakes . . . [*spits*].

Backstage, in the dressing room, Jolene is standing in her striking new rigout singing along with Jim Bob who's playing over a tinny tannoy, and applying yet another coat of Carmine Lip Gloss to her already dazzling mouth.

Billie opens the dressing door and eyes Frank on the phone down the corridor.

Frank [*On phone*] . . . lemme talk to Tamara, I've just went an' swallowed that murder story of hers . . . [*spits*].

Jolene] So?

Billie closes the door and looks at Jolene.

Billie] So I spoke with the management.

Jolene] And?

Billie] We're on at the drinks interval.

Billie's eyes sparkle.

Jolene] Aw, well done, McPhail. I thought this was meant to be wur big chance?

Jolene turns away in disgust.

Billie] It still is wur big chance,

there's a wee guy sittin' right in the front row wi' a leather coat an' a pony-tail . . .

She weighs her words carefully.

Billie] . . . he's smokin' a Gooloise.

Boyle's fish van is trundling along the wet Wishaw road, the wipers are slapping in time to 'You are my Sunshine' which is playing over the radio.
    Boyle eyes Cissie.

Boyle] Stop lookin' at us like that . . . I'm doin' the pair of you a big favour gettin' the boy out the country. [*Over shoulder*] Y'awright back there, Dorwood?

Cissie] 'Fraid he was goin' to spew up the truth on his sick bed, is that it?

She turns to the grill opening behind the front seats.

Cissie [*Loudly*] What possessed you to go along with this farcical notion! Not only have you scuppered any chance of me gettin' my son back, you're goin' to wind up gettin' another five years, ya numbskull!

Boyle [*Over shoulder*] Don't listen to her, ole buddy . . . this time next

week you're gonnae find yourself on the Costa Blanca doin' 'China Doll' for one of the best bands to break outta Belfast in a blue moon.

Cissie [*Over shoulder*] I'd take the five years . . .

There is a moan from Dorwood in the back of the van.

Cissie [*To Boyle*] . . . he's just had a brain scan, ya scumbag!

Boyle] An I've just had a fried egg roll on top of a nervous stomach, quit screamin' at us!

Cissie] Aw, naw . . .

Boyle] What?

Up ahead in the road is a line of disembodied luminescent stripes and waving lights. They loom out of the murky dark on the motorway approach road.

Boyle] That's aw we need . . . [*Over shoulder*] . . . don't want to alarm you, good buddy, but we're comin' up to a line of berrs at a road block . . . [*To Cissie*] . . . any funny business an' you're dead meat, darlin'.

Boyle slows the van down and stops at the road block. He winds the window down and sticks his head out as a policeman moves towards them waving his torch.

Boyle] S'up, you lost somethin', you guys?

Boyle shields his face as the policeman's torch sweeps the cab.

Policeman] D'you want to turn that racket down a bit?

Boyle] D'you want to get that searchlight out ma face?

Policeman] Turn it down!

Cissie reaches over and turns the radio volume down low.

Policeman] You didnae happen to pick up any hitchhikers on your travels, did you?

His torch beam plays over Cissie in the passenger seat.

Boyle] Just the wife here, we're goin' to the Stations of the Cross in Carluke . . . what's all this in aid of?

Policeman] S'your back doors unlocked?

Boyle] Sure, help yourself . . .

Cissie [*Involuntarily*] Aw, Jesus . . .

She puts a hand to her face as Boyle punches her hard on the thigh.

Cissie] . . . ow!

The policeman returns to shine his torch into the cab.

Policeman] D'you say somethin', love?

Boyle] Not me, pal.

Boyle turns to Cissie.

Boyle] Y'awright, sweetheart?

He rubs his hand along Cissie's thigh.

Cissie [*Tartly*] I'm fine.

Cissie knocks Boyle's hand from her leg.
He turns and leans his head out of the window.

Boyle [*Confidentially to policeman*] Fine, she says . . . just had a bone marra transplant to her hip-joint . . . quack reckons that's her showbiz career curtailed . . . used to dance wi' the Muppets.

Policeman] Switch your engine off.

The policeman moves around to the rear of the van.
There are now several other vehicles that have been stopped and the occupants are being questioned by other police officers.

Boyle [*Loudly, to anyone*] Some how-d'you-do this, eh?

At the back of the fish van the policeman grabs the rear door handle and hauls one half of the double doors open.

Policeman] Bloody hell . . .

The policeman takes a step

backwards, his hand to his face, as the acrid stench of dead fish hits his nostrils.

Boyle [*Loudly, to anyone*] Any you drivers know if there's a ten o'clock Mass in Larkhall the night?

Unwilling to get any closer, the policeman gives the van interior a cursory sweep with his torch, and satisfies himself that it's empty of passengers, before kicking the door shut with the toe of his boot.
  Dorwood, crouched behind the unopened half of the van doors, puts a hand to his injured head as the other door bangs shut.

Policeman] Right, get this stinkin' heap outta here . . .

Boyle smiles to himself as he turns the ignition key and the engine coughs into life.
  The policeman comes up alongside the cab.

Policeman] . . . C'mon, move.

Boyle lets the clutch out, and the fish van lurches off, only to stall some five yards up the road. Dorwood and the crates in the back are thrown forward in the dark.

Dorwood [*On hands and knees*] C'mon, move!

The engine revs, splutters, and dies . . .
  Beads of sweat break out on Boyle's brow as he turns the ignition key again. The engine wow-wows ominously.

Cissie] C'mon, move . . .

Horns begin to beep behind them.

Boyle [*Loudly*] Awright, shurrup wi' the horns!

He tries the ignition key again as the policeman comes up alongside the cab.

Policeman [*To Boyle*] You are bein' a right bloody nuisance, you are . . . [*To drivers behind*] Shurrup! [*To Boyle*] You got a handle, yeh?
Boyle] Handle? Aye . . . Fraser. How?

He turns the ignition key once more.

Cissie] A startin' handle, ya mug.
Boyle] Aw. [*To policeman*] Yeh, there should be one in the b . . .

The starter motor suddenly catches, and the engine roars impressively.

Boyle] . . . I don't believe it.

Policeman] Right, Fraser . . . beat it.

The fish van weaves its way between the police vehicles at the road block and sets off along the motorway.

Boyle] Eeeeeeeeeeeeeha!

Cissie peers anxiously through the grill opening in the back wall of the cab.

Cissie] Yeh, dead jammy but what if that cop'd had to hunt in the back for the startin' hand . . .

She turns her head as Boyle reaches under the dashboard and produces an enormous lethal-looking navy Colt revolver.

Cissie] . . . aw, my God.

Boyle] Good job for him I got her goin', innit?

He brandishes the revolver in front of the grill.

Boyle [*Over shoulder*] Never guess where this turned up, ole buddy . . .

Cissie] Stop wavin' that about.

Boyle [*Over shoulder*] . . . wrapped inside a lassie's scarf on top of a wardrobe in your apartment . . . 'much did we give thon mad guy

for it . . . four quid? [*To Cissie*] Four quid.

The van inches over into the adjoining lane.

Cissie] Watch out!

She grabs the steering wheel and brings the van back into line as a car, horn blaring, overtakes them on the outside.

Boyle] Flang in three live rounds along with it, as I recall . . .

He holds the revolver up and squints into the chamber.

Cissie [*Loudly, to grill*] What in God's name were you doin' with a gun, ya lunatic!

Boyle spins the chamber against his leg and brings the gun up to Cissie's temple.

Boyle] . . . one for him, one for you . . .

Cissie [*Defiantly*] Yeh, go on, I dare you.

Boyle cocks the hammer.

Boyle] . . . an' one for Junior.

Cissie's face remains impassive.

Cissie] You utter shit.

Boyle [*Over shoulder, to Dorwood*] Ho . . . d'you hear what she's cryin' us, ole buddy? [*To Cissie*] That isnae very ladylike, sweetheart . . .

His voice takes on a harder edge.

Boyle] . . . wouldnae take me that long to get up to Aberdeen an' back in this jalopy so don't get surly, d'you hear?

He presses the gun barrel against the side of Cissie's head.

Boyle [*Over shoulder*] Remind me to let you have the wee fulla's address . . . you can drop him a poscard from wherever you happen to be on this European tour with Jim Bob . . . [*To Cissie*] Don't worry, he's wi' a nice family . . . foster-da's a telephone engineer . . . foster-ma's a total abstainer . . . there's two older kids an' a spaniel . . . 'Trixie'. Couldnae be happier. C'mon, smile . . .

He de-cocks the revolver and removes it from Cissie's temple.

Boyle] . . . I got your man out the jile, didn't I?

There is a moan from Dorwood in the back.

Boyle] Beg your pardon . . . hospital.

He sticks the gun into the waistband of his Wranglers . . . and winces slightly as he does so.

Boyle [*Over shoulder*] 'Much did we say, old pal . . . two grand, was it? [*To Cissie*] Two grand . . . cash.

Dorwood's face appears at the grill opening.

Dorwood] D'you think we could stop for a minute? I don't think I'm feelin' too hot . . .

Boyle] Relax, we've no' got far to go.

Dorwood [*To Cissie*] Did that doll get in touch with you about ma redundancy money?

Cissie stares straight ahead.

Cissie] What redundancy money?

Dorwood] The doll off the *Echo* . . .

Dorwood goes into a coughing fit.

Dorwood] . . . aw, God . . .

Boyle [*To Chrissie*] Whereabouts were you headed anyhow? [*Over shoulder*] You want to keep an eye on this little lady of yours, ole buddy . . .

Dorwood [*Between coughs*] . . . I planked it inside thon radio.

Boyle] . . . out cruisin' the highways in her best duds while you're laid up in a hospital bed gettin' the last sacraments?

Dorwood [*Feebly*] . . . know the one I mean?

Boyle [*To Cissie*] That just isnae tactful, darlin' . . .

Dorwood [*Weakening*] I know I shoulda told you about it . . .

His face disappears from the grill.

Dorwood] . . . but I wouldnae've got legal aid.

Dorwood goes into an enfeebling coughing bout.

Boyle] That is one sick boy back there . . . yessiree, one very sick boy.

Frank is still at the pay-phone in the Ponderosa Club.

Frank [*On phone*] . . . naw . . . 'wood', Tamara . . . as in 'or would you rather be a fish?' . . . the guy that fell off the roof, I was readin' your piece in the taxi but you didnae mention what hospital he was . . .

He hears continuous beep-beeps as the pay-phone runs out of money again.

Frank] . . . dammit . . .

There is applause behind him as Jim Bob and the Wild Bunch finish a number. Frank searches frantically through his coat pockets.

Frank [*On phone, through beeps*] . . .

I'm tryin' to find out if Cis . . . if his wife . . . naw, I cannae tell you where I am . . . it doesnae accept incomin' calls any . . .

The line breaks . . .

Frank] . . . how . . . bugger.

Frank gives up his fruitless search for dough, hangs up the receiver, and leans his forehead against the wall. Behind him Jim Bob launches into 'Tennessee Waltz'.

Down the corridor in the dressing room Billie is sitting with the Dobro on her lap singing along with Jim Bob on the tannoy. There is no sign of Jolene.

Billie [*Singing*] ' . . . when an old friend I happened to see . . . introduced him to ma darlin' and as they were waltzin', ma friend stole ma sweetheart from me . . .'

Jolene enters the dressing room.

Billie [*Singing*] . . . 'I remember the night . . .'

Jolene] I thought you said the wee guy in the front row was from one of the music papers?

Billie] Well, that's what I . . .

Jolene [*Angrily*] He's a wumman's hair stylist, I've just checked. See you, Billie McPhail!

She tears off her new blouson and chucks it across the room.

Billie] What you doin'? We're on after this number . . .

Jolene stalks off towards the walk-in closet, goes in and slams the door.

Billie] Jolene?

Jolene [*From closet, muffled*] Lea' me alone!

The Wild Bunch go into a fiddle-led instrumental break on the tinny tannoy.
Frank is still standing in the corridor with his forehead pressed against the wall next to the pay-phone.
The Tall Cowpoke ambles along the corridor, opening doors and peering inside.

Tall Cowpoke [*Loudly*] Y'err, Roxanne? [*To Frank*] You huvnae saw a burd wi' a T-shirt an' a biro waunnerin' aboot backstage, huv ye, pal? [*Loudly*] Y'err, honeybunch?

He opens the door nearest Frank and sticks his head inside.

Tall Cowpoke] Woops.

He closes the door.

Tall Cowpoke [*To Frank*] T-shirt's goat Dave Dee, Dozey, Wozey, Mick'n'Dick oan the front . . . biro belangs tae the shoap . . .

He wanders off along the corridor.
Frank heaves a sigh, straightens up, and heads towards the emergency exit doors leading to the car park. Hands thrust forlornly in his raincoat pockets, he has a dirty great smudge on his forehead.

Tall Cowpoke [*Muffled*] Y'err Roxanne?

Ralph Henderson is at the wheel of his white BMW driving along to Wishaw. Tonto sits in the passenger seat next to him.

Henderson [*On carphone*] . . . no, stay put, I'm on my way there n . . . don't shout at me, I've just spent a fruitless ninety minutes up to my armpits in dead crayfish!

Tonto leans forward in the passenger seat and peers through the windscreen.

Henderson [*On carphone*] Never mind what for . . .

Tonto takes a pair of shades from his top pocket and slips them on. He leans forward and peers through the windscreen.

Henderson [*On carphone*] . . . did you book us a table at that Italian joint?

Tonto gives Henderson a nudge and points through the windscreen.

Henderson [*On carphone*] Okay, okay, I'll do it . . . talk to you later.

A policeman waves down the approaching BMW at the road block. Henderson lowers the window.

Henderson] 'Evening, officer . . . Ralph Henderson . . . Melon, Brolly and Henderson . . . what seems to be the problem?

The policeman bends down and flashes his torch into the car.

Tamara MacAskill replaces the carphone, draws a scarlet fingernail carefully underneath a moist eye. She glances at her reflection in the rear-view mirror, sniffs, checks her watch, and picks up a portable tape recorder from the front passenger seat of her car.

There is a light tap on the windscreen.

Tamara glances up and sees Frank McClusky's face pressed against the window. She draws back startled.

Tamara] Wah!

Frank leans down to the driver's window of the parked radio car.

Frank and Tamara [*Together*] What're you doing here? I've just been talking to you . . .

Frank] . . . at the office, naw?

Tamara] . . . God, what a fright.

She sniffs and pushes the car door open.

Frank] There's me huntin' through ma pockets for loose coins when I could just . . .

Tamara clambers out of the car clutching her tape recorder.

Tamara [*Interrupting*] I'm waiting to interview this Irish chap for the ten o'clock news . . . my God, you look awful . . .

She looks Frank up and down.

Frank] I'm on the run, Tamara . . .

Tamara] . . . I mean, you don't look too terrific at the best of times but . . . ha!

Frank] 'Ha'?

Tamara] What on earth have you got on your feet!

Frank's eyes follow Tamara's.

Frank] Aw, these? These're Dorwood's.

Tamara] Oh. I thought for a second they were cowboy boots, I was going to ask what got into you.

She fumbles with her car keys.

Frank] Allow me.

Frank takes the keys and locks the radio car door.

Frank and Tamara [*Together*] You don't happen to know . . .

Frank] . . . know what?

Tamara] . . . no, no, carry on, what were you going to ask?

She discovers that the tape recorder mike lead has got inexplicably and inextricably fankled in Frank's Burberry belt.

Frank] You don't happen to know when Big Gordon's gettin' buried, do you?

They set off across the car park together, Tamara puzzling over the problem with her mike lead.

Tamara] When who's getting what?

Frank] Gordon Smart . . . guy they fished out the Clyde . . .

Tamara squints across the car park at Jim Bob's trailer.

Tamara [*Interrupting*] Does that look like a 'Wendy-bagel' to you? Sorry, what were you saying?

She stops and grapples with the mike lead and the raincoat belt.

Frank] . . . his Maw was a cripple . . . turned up at the school prize giving one year in the back of the boy Ragazzo's ice-cream motor . . .

Tamara] You don't happen to know any Italian restaurants around here?

Frank] . . . Big Gordon won himself a Palgrave's *Golden Treasury* . . .

Tamara] There used to be one in the High Street with venetian blinds but it's all boarded up.

Frank] . . . Libo Ragazzo half-inched it out his toilet bag . . . Fraser Boyle fashioned a one to ten thou pop-up model of Graceland outta *The Cottar's Saturday Night* . . . I'd quite like to be at his funeral.

Tamara] Lago di Something? . . . He's got this thing about Ossobucco.

Frank] Lago di Lucca . . . I devoted a half-column to it last month, guy sent me a death threat through the post. Who's got this 'thing' about . . .

Tamara] Ralph.

Frank] Ralph?

Tamara] Spent our entire honeymoon stuffing himself.

Frank] Aw, that Ralph? Thought you an' him went to Michigan, naw?

Tamara] Is this belt stitched to the back?

Frank] I'm only goin' by what Trish in Copy told everybody . . .

Tamara] Damn!

She sucks a broken fingernail.

Frank] . . . I used to know a Ralph, only this guy called himself Raif, like in Vaughan-Williams . . . nice big chap . . . tone deaf . . . we got arrested together at university . . . last I heard he went into the army, got posted to Northern Ireland . . . havenae seen him since . . . I think that belt's stitched to the back . . . is it?

A young man and his girlfriend come round the corner and peer through the front door of the Bar-L into the darkened interior.

A voice comes out of the shadows.

Voice] Thur shut.

A man's unattractive features glow in the shadows as he drags hard on a cigarette butt. He flicks the butt away and limps out under the street lamp.

Girlfriend] Their pokey hat's on.

Limping man] Where?

The limping man and the young man step into the street and look up at the Bar-L roof. Ragazzo's pokey hat glows fitfully against the black velvet of the night sky.

Young man] Aw, aye, so it is.

Limping man] Soon fix that, hen.

The limping man draws back an arm with a half-brick on the end of it. The young man and his girlfriend look up, their eyes following the flight path of the missile.

There is a crash, followed by the sound of a burglar alarm going off.

In the car park of the Ponderosa, Tamara, with Frank in tow on the end of her microphone lead, walks over to the Winnebago and rattles the door.

A bouncer appears at the door of the club, opens the door and pins it back.

MC [*From club*] Thank you, ladies an' gen'lemen, that's your refreshments interlude right now . . .

Frank [*To Tamara*] What time you goin' back to Glasgow at?

A sweating Jim Bob and his band tear out of the club towards the Winnebago.
   Tamara whirls round and points her microphone at them.

Tamara] Hi . . . Tamara MacAskill, Radio Kelvin, did someone give you a ring about a possible interview regarding Jim Bob's alleged involvement with the INLA?

Frank pretends to be a passer-by.
   The Tall Cowpoke wanders by, still looking for Roxanne.
   Inside the dressing room Billie listens to the MC over the tannoy. Jolene is still hidden in the closet.

MC] . . . your pub next door here does some very tasty Kentucky ham vol-a-vongs . . .

Billie [*To closet*] We're on, Jolene!

On a slip road, off the motorway, Fraser Boyle's fish van sits, bonnet up, with its engine smoking.
   Boyle has removed his jacket, rolled up his sleeves, and is leaning over the mudguard to investigate the problem.
   Boyle straightens up and removes the navy Colt from his waistband. He sets it down nearby before leaning over the engine again.
   Cissie is sitting in the van behind the steering wheel.

Dorwood] Yeh, so you keep sayin' but I was goin' bananas in that joint . . .

Cissie [*Over shoulder*] Are you callin' me a liar?

Dorwood's knuckles whiten as he pushes his face up against the grill.

Dorwood] What about all these letters I've been gettin'?

Cissie] What letters?

Dorwood] In green biro! You have so been seein' guys. I can tell!

Cissie] Och, away an' don't be stupit.

Boyle [*Loudly, from under the bonnet*] Okay, turn over!

Cissie reaches for the ignition key.

Dorwood] See if I find out . . .

The rest of his words are drowned out by the chug-chug of the engine before it coughs and dies.

Dorwood [*Continues*] . . . an' that isnae just an empty threat, right!

Billie appears at the entrance of the Ponderosa, she casts around the car park in panic. She spots Frank over by the Winnebago with his ear to the door. She rushes across to him.

Billie] C'mon, you're wanted . . .

She grabs hold of Frank and tries hauling him away from the trailer.

Frank [*Sotto voce*] Beat it, Shorty, can you not see I'm tied up!

Billie] C'mon, I said!

She grabs Frank by the scruff of his shirt collar and pulls him out of his belted Burberry like a caterpillar from a cocoon.

Frank] Ooooooooooooooow!

Billie drags Frank bodily across the tarmac leaving his raincoat dangling by the microphone lead from the Winnebago door.

The white BMW peels off the motorway, and takes the road to Wishaw.

A short way along they see a fish van parked by the verge. A man steps into the road, and waves his arms.

Tonto leans forward in his seat and peers out through the windscreen.

Tonto] We don't want any fish, dae we?

Fraser Boyle's face contorts into a silently cursing mask as the BMW sweeps past.

Tonto swivels round to look back down the road.

Henderson] Lago di Lucca . . .

Henderson passes a slim address book to Tonto.

Henderson] . . . quiet table for two . . . 10 o'clock.

Tonto takes the address book, picks up the carphone, and punches in a number.

Tonto] What aboot the wife, she no' comin', naw?

Billie has just arrived on the Ponderosa stage. There are five patrons, presumably teetotallers, dotted around the room, all looking badly in need of cheering up.

Billie [*Into mike*] Howdy . . .

The hair stylist with a ponytail and a leather coat sits in the front row munching a hotdog from a doyley.

Billie [*Turning head*] . . . is this mike on? [*Into mike*] Howdy, Wishaw . . .

She runs her plectrum across the

144

guitar strings.

Billie] . . . I'd like to introduce you to a coupla McPhail Sisters' Friends this evening . . . would you welcome, on slide guitar . . . Mister Frank McCusker.

Frank is busy hunting for a socket in the amplifier to plug the Dobro jack into.

Frank] McClusky.

He disappears behind the amp.

Billie] And replacing Jolene Jowett on vocals . . . [*To Roxanne*] . . . What's your second name again?

Roxanne leans forward from the stage so that the hair stylist in the front row can finger her tresses.

Frank [*Behind amp*] McClusky!
Billie [*Into mike*] . . . Rexene McClusky.

Bille hits the opening chords of 'Silver Threads and Golden Needles'.

Frank [*To anyone*] Any you guys seen a bottleneck?
Roxanne [*To hair stylist*] Naw, no' like hurs . . . somethin' stylish, yeh?

She crosses to the mike.

Billie] Thanks a bunch. [*To Frank*] In G.

Roxanne launches into the opening verse.

Roxanne's voice comes belting over the tannoy into the dressing room backstage. The closet door creaks open, and Jolene appears, eating her way through a packet of biscuits.
She stares at the tannoy.

Jolene] Ya cheeky bitch . . .

A fountain of digestive biscuit crumbs arcs across the room.

Jolene] . . . that's ma number!

Boyle is still fiddling about under the bonnet of the immobilised fish van.
There is no response from the cab, and Boyle emerges, his hands blackened with grease.

Boyle [*Loudly*] Try that, I said!

There is still no response.
Boyle takes a couple of paces away from the engine and looks into the cab. There is no sign of Cissie. He gallops round to the back of the van. The rear doors are gaping wide. But there is no sign of Dorwood apart from a trail of bandages snaking across the verge. Boyle spins round and runs out into the road. His head swivels this way and that. He reaches for the revolver at his waist . . . and

panics. Then he remembers and races back to the van. There is no sign of the navy Colt where he left it.

Boyle] Aw, naw . . .

He strikes his palm on his forehead leaving a big black oily mark.

Cissie is standing alone at the side of the Wishaw road keeping a lookout for oncoming cars.

Cissie [*To Dorwood, in bushes*] Keep down, they're hardly goin' to pull up for a guy in his PJs . . . you could be an escaped lunatic.

She steps out into the road to thumb down the approaching headlights.

Cissie [*To herself*] What'm I sayin'? You are an escaped lunatic.

There is a roar as several vehicles race past her.
   A shivering Dorwood emerges from the roadside undergrowth and draws a flimsy hospital blanket round his shoulders.

Dorwood [*To disappearing tail lights*] Aye, cheers, pal . . . wait to you're on the run an' aw you've got on your feet's a perra bedsocks! [*To Cissie*] You might've thought to bring us ma new boots instead of

these useless items . . .

Dorwood looks down at his sodden feet and sneezes.

Cissie] I wasn't to know you were goin' walkabout, was I?

Dorwood] Me neither . . . one minute I'm at death's doorstep, next minute Fraser Boyle's got his leg over the winda-sill an' him an' I's makin' a break for . . . [*Looks around*] . . . where in God's name . . . [*Sneezes*] . . . are we?

Cissie peels her jacket off.

Cissie] Here . . .

She places the jacket around Dorwood's shoulders.

Dorwood] What you doin'? Get that offa me.

He shrugs Cissie's jacket off his shoulders on to the ground. Cissie looks down at the jacket, and then up at Dorwood.
   Cissie bends down, picks up the jacket and replaces it around her husband's shoulders.

Dorwood] Somethin' up wi' your hearin'?

He shrugs Cissie's jacket on to the ground again.

Cissie] Pick that up.

Dorwood] You pick it up, it's your . . . (*Sneezes*).

Cissie] D'you want to catch pneumonia? Pick that up when you're told.

Dorwood] Away to . . . (*Sneezes*) . . . aaaah, ma head.

Cissie] Quit moanin' about your stupit head an' get that jacket . . .

Dorwood [*Interrupting*] Moanin'? Who's moanin'? All I've done is bite the bullet ever since I dove Christ-knows-how-many feet offa that roof! (*Sneezes*) Ahyah . . .

Cissie] Bite the bullet? Don't make me laugh, you've done nothin' but feel sorry for yourself ever since you got arrested . . . an' you shouldn't've been on the bloody roof, you should've been in your room!

Dorwood] Cell, Cissie . . . they don't put you in a room, they lock you up in a . . . (*Sneezes*) . . . cell!

Cissie] Yeh, whatever . . . just pick up the jacket an' . . .

Dorwood [*Interrupting*] There were three other galoots in there along wi' us . . .

He starts pacing to and fro in a vain effort to get warm.

Cissie] The jacket, Dorwood.

Dorwood] . . . One for stickin' a bottle-opener through his girlfriend's neck, one for sawin' the thumbs off a security guard, an' the other one was . . . [*Sneezes*] . . . bloody Dwane. One toilet, four guys . . . it was worse than bein' on the road, for Christ's . . .

He turns to find himself staring down a gun barrel.

Dorwood [*Tailing off*] . . . sake. What the hell're you doin' with . . .

Cissie [*Interrupting*] Pick up the jacket, Dorwood.

She waves the gun at him.

Cissie] Pick up the jacket unless you want to die!

Dorwood reaches down and picks up the jacket.

Dorwood] Yeh, go on, I . . . [*Sneezes*] . . . I dare you.

Cissie] From exposure, ya nitwit! Right, get it on . . . c'mon, hurry up!

Dorwood] You're just out to humiliate me, that's what you're out to do . . .

He puts his arms through the sleeves

Cissie] What're you talkin' about, humiliate you? I'm tryin' to

147

prevent you from gettin' pleurisy, ya . . .

Dorwood] This's a lassie's jacket!

Cissie] It's a what?

Dorwood] This! It's been made for a lassie . . . look at it!

Cissie] What the hell does it matter who it was made for as long as . . .

Dorwood [*Interrupting*] A helluva bloody lot, it matters! If this ever gets near the papers the fans're gonnae go . . . [*Sneezes*] . . . the fans're gonnae . . . [*Sneezes*] . . . the fans're gonnae go mental!

He pulls the jacket on and stands there.

Dorwood] They'll crucify us . . . look at the state of me . . . aw I need's a shoulder bag an' wur album's out the charts for evermore!

Cissie] Mental, did you say?

Dorwood] Yeh, awright, Miss Intellect, so they don't aw read wee print an' tune into Channel Four movies, but the one thing they do do is go out an' buy Country music secure in the knowledge that Hank Snow isnae gonnae stroll onstage at the Grand Ole Opry in a wumman's evenin' gown!

Cissie] I thought Hank Snow was dead?

Dorwood] Willie bloody Nelson, well! Don't get smart . . .

Cissie] Och, I give up . . . do you seriously mean to tell me that you would rather catch pleurisy than . . .

Dorwood] Too bloody right, I would!

Dorwood gets the jacket half-off when he is overtaken by a violent sneezing fit.

Cissie] That's right . . . die, ya dope!

Dorwood [*Recovering*] Yeh, that would suit you just fine, wouldn't it?

Cissie] Too bloody right, it would!

Dorwood struggles manfully to escape from the jacket, but he is hampered by the hospital blanket underneath and by the tightness of its lassie's sleeves.

Dorwood] Well, I hate to disappoint you, sweetheart, but you ain't gonnae be left a single parent for some considerable . . . [*Loud sneeze*] . . . ah, Jesus, ma napper . . .

Still trapped in the jacket, Dorwood lurches forward and leans himself against Cissie, exhausted. Cissie looks down at him and for the first time she sees a lurid gash in the middle of a shaven spot on Dorwood's skull.

Cissie] Aw, my God . . .

She sticks the revolver inside her shirt and reaches out to touch the ugly wound.

Dorwood [*Bent over*] Don't touch it!

Cissie] I wasn't goin' to touch it . . . 'many stitches did you get? One, two, three . . .

Dorwood] Forty-seven . . . naw forty-nine.

Cissie [*Peering close*] It's not very neat, is it?

Dorwood] They didnae get a seamstress in to do it, naw!

Cissie] It looks awful sore . . .

Dorwood] It is awful sore! I havenae slept a wink since it happened, kept wakin' up wi' the skitters.

Cissie] Kept wakin' up with the what?

Dorwood] The skitters! In case they started clubbin' us again . . .

Cissie] In case who started . . .

Dorwood [*Interrupting*] . . . didnae have a mark on us . . . fell on top of the screw that was tryin' to talk me down, shattered his pelvis, broke all his top teeth . . . his pals just couldnae see the funny side, started knockin' lumps outta ma . . . ach, what d'you care?

Cissie] Talk sense, ya dummy, of course, I care! We'll sue!

Dorwood] Sue?

Cissie] Sue!

Dorwood] Sue who?

Cissie] The Governor, the prison authorities, the Home Office!

Dorwood] Don't talk romantic, it's ma word against theirs, innit? 'Prisoner was resisting recapture, m'lord . . . the officers were obliged to exercise restraint . . .'

Cissie] Restraint? They've smashed your skull in!

Dorwood [*Loudly*] I know they've smashed ma sk . . . ooooow!

He holds on to his head.

Cissie] There must've been witnesses that saw what happened.

Dorwood] Yeh . . . Dwane . . . I clocked his wee beady eyes keekin' out into the playground just before I went under.

Cissie] We'll get him to testify. If he can identify the lousy pigs that . . .

Dorwood [*Interrupting*] Dwane Devlin? Dwane couldnae identify himself in the mirror if you gave him his passport pitcher. [*Softly*] Ohyah . . .

Cissie] I thought you an' Dwane were quite close?

Dorwood] Never trust a guy with a tattoo of Farley Granger on his bum . . .

His body starts to heave.

Dorwood] . . . I used to lend that swine shurts an' everythin' . . .

Cissie [*Tenderly*] C'mere . . .

She holds him close

Dorwood [*Between sobs*] . . . got them back, cuffs were all frayed, collars were absolutely manky.

Cissie] Did you really get the last sacraments, yeh?

Dorwood wipes his eyes on Cissie's shirt collar.

Dorwood] Did I what?

Cissie] The last sacraments? Fraser Boyle said you'd got . . .

Dorwood [*Interrupting*] 'Course I got the last sacraments, they thought I was gonnae snuff it, didn't they! [*Sneezes*] Ooooooooooow!

Cissie] Try not to sneeze.

Dorwood] Aw, yeh, sound advice . . . thanks a bloody . . . [*Sneezes*] ahyah, bastart!

Cissie] First thing we have to do is to get you out of that wet stuff an' into some proper clothes . . .

Dorwood] Aye, very good . . . what d'you suggest, poppin' into the nearest Co-operative outfitters an' pickin' somethin' off the rail? We're in the middle of Nowhere Gulch, for Christ's sake!

Cissie] Don't raise your voice, you'll only aggravate that gash . . s'not itchy, is it?

Dorwood] Naw, just very painful! Aaaaah . . .

Cissie] Don't worry, it'll get itchy . . . d'you remember when Thomas's buggy turned over an' . . . [*She stops herself*].

Dorwood] Naw, I don't . . . was this when you were hittin' the sauce, yeh?

Cissie [*Looking away*] He only ever had a wee tiny scar . . . just here . . .

She puts a finger to her hair, just behind her ear.

Cissie] . . . shaped like a tortoise . . . [*Quickly*] . . . d'you want to start walkin'?

Dorwood] Walkin'?

Cissie] Not much point in hangin' about here, Fraser Boyle could be along in that clapped-out fish truck any minute . . .

She pulls the jacket up over Dorwood's shoulders.

Dorwood] Yeh, what is it with you an' Fraser? I always thought you an' him got on like a house on fire.

Cissie] S'that what he told you?

She fastens Dorwood's jacket buttons.

Dorwood] Listen, if it hadnae've been for Fraser Boyle I wouldnae be standin' here right now.

Cissie] Exactly. C'mon . . .

She starts walking Dorwood along the road.

Dorwood] Didnae relish handin' him a measly two grand for gettin' us out the country, s'that what it is? Eh? S'that what it is, Cissie?

Cissie] How in God's name was Fraser Boyle goin' to get you out the country . . .

Dorwood] Simple . . .

Cissie] . . . he cannae even get his motor started!

Dorwood] . . . one of the Wild Bunch lends us an Irish passport, I get ma snap taken, we hand the lot over to a guy called Cherokee George, George does the business, 'Jim Bob's your uncle' . . . Naw, listen, listen . . . their Hawaiian guitar player's wife's expectin', he'll be quite happy to hop it back to Derry while I fly outta Hamburg for the States . . . it's all arranged. All you have to do is hand over the two Gs to Boyle, change the rest of ma redundancy dough into travellers' cheques, stick them in an envelope an' . . .

Cissie [*Interrupting*] Promise me somethin', Dorwood . . .

Dorwood] Don't worry . . . soon as I hit Nashville I'm gonnae mail you out two 'plane tickets . . . one for you, one for . . .

Cissie [*Interrupting*] . . . naw, somethin' else, Dorwood.

Dorwood] Yeh, what?

Cissie] Promise me you'll resist the urge to pen the definitive work on British constitutional history.

Dorwood] British constitutional what?

Cissie] They don't have Irish passports in Derry, they have United Kingdom passports, same as you an' I have got!

Dorwood] Aw, yeh? So how come I'm to give Fraser Boyle two thousand quid for gettin' us . . .

Dorwood stops walking.

Cissie [*Interrupting*] An' somethin' else you ought to know . . . you don't have any 'redundancy dough' so that's the entire enterprise knocked on the head.

She starts walking Dorwood along the road again.

Dorwood] What d'you mean, I don't have any redundancy d . . . [*Sneezes*].

Cissie] 'Cos I burnt it . . . pick your feet up . . .

Dorwood] . . . it's tucked inside thon Gene Autry . . . [*Stops dead*] What'd you say?

Cissie] . . . your feet . . . pick them up.

Dorwood] You burnt it!

Cissie] Just the money, your Gene Autry radio's quite safe, I put it in the tea-chest along with . . .

Dorwood [*Interrupting*] Eighteen thousand quid . . . you actually burnt eighteen . . .

Cissie [*Interrupting*] It's your own fault, you should've told me about it . . . I presumed it was the proceeds from . . .

Cissie turns round as Dorwood drops to his knees and starts beating his head on the tarmac.

Cissie] . . . stop that, ya headbanger!

She grabs Dorwood by the scruff of his lassie's jacket and pulls him into an upright kneeling position. She can see his blood-flecked face in the lights of the approaching cars.

Dorwood [*Ferociously*] Waaaaaaaaaaaaaaaa . . . choo!

On the Ponderosa Club stage Billie and Roxanne are harmonising sweetly on 'These Two Empty Arms'. Jolene stands at one side of the stage, a little apart from the others, with her accordion strapped to her chest, and a face like fizz.

Jolene [*To Billie*] Away, ya two-faced get!

Frank, bent over his amplifier, glances across at Jolene.

Jolene [*To Frank*] Not you . . . her, there. [*To Billie*] Yeh, you, ya insect!

Roxanne [*Between verses*] S'up wi' yur associate?

Billie] I forgot to bring her poncho.

Frank shuffles over to Jolene and starts fingering her blouson.

Jolene [*To Frank*] . . . go on, have a guess . . . seventy-nine fifty, reduced from three hundred an' eighty-four, an' she's got the gall to invite a two-pound T-shirt in a Sixties hairdo onstage to do all ma numbers? . . . She can sing nane, McPhail!

Billie and Jolene's voices drift through the air and out into the dark car park outside.

Tonto, who has been examining the Burberry's sleeves sticking out of the Winnebago door, steps smartly back into the shadows as the door is opened and Tamara is 'shown out'.

Tamara [*To outlaw*] All right, all right, I'm going, there's no need to shove . . . ow!

The outlaw rips the tape reel out of

the recorder and hurls the machine across the car park. Tamara stumbles across the tarmac to retrieve it.

Tonto slips out of the shadows and into Jim Bob's trailer as Tamara gathers up the tape recorder and hurries across the car park towards the white BMW, with Frank's discarded raincoat dragging along behind.

Onstage, Frank has accidentally solved the Dobro amplification problem, and takes off on a shaky bottleneck solo that gains in confidence (if not immediately in polish) as it intertwines with Jolene's accordion on the instrumental break in 'These Two Empty Arms'.

Billie [*To Jolene*] Okay, so Ry Cooder, he isnae, but he's got wee Desmond tanked.

The Tall Cowpoke and Drew materialise beside the hair stylist in the front row.

Jolene] Yeh, if we play wur cards right we might get a free perm . . . chuck tryin' to sook in, McPhail.

Roxanne [*To Tall Cowpoke*] S'up wi' your face?

Tall Cowpoke [*To hair stylist*] Did you gi'e hur an estimate furra herrdo?

Frank's raincoat is now to be seen

hanging from the mike lead outside the rear passenger door of the white BMW. Inside the car Tamara is gesticulating at Ralph Henderson.

Tamara] For heaven's sake, you're a solicitor, Ralph, there must be something you can do . . . those tapes are Radio Kelvin property.

The carphone rings, and Henderson snatches at the receiver.

Henderson [*Into carphone*] Yes?

In a phone booth near the Bar-L a limping man, covered all over in a fine layer of white powder, is trying to talk into the upside-down pay-phone receiver.

Limping man [*Into phone*] Hey . . . [*Sniffs*] . . . whooo!

Cissie and Dorwood have finally reached the Ponderosa Club car park. A shivering Dorwood crouches behind Tamara's radio car as Cissie surveys the scene from its shadow. Roxanne, the Tall Cowpoke and Drew all wander across the tarmac arguing.

Roxanne] Whit'd ye go an' drag us away fur?

Cissie ducks out of sight beside Dorwood.

Roxanne] I wisnae especially wantin' a vol-a-vong . . .

Dorwood [*To Cissie*] Bring us somethin' to eat, will you?

Cissie [*Sotto voce*] Shhhhhhhh!

The Tall Cowpoke, Drew, and Roxanne make their way past the radio car towards a nearby pub.

Tall Cowpoke [*To Drew*] Did you get that biro affa hur?

Cissie eases herself cautiously upright after they have passed by.

Cissie [*Sotto voce, to Dorwood*] Wait here, okay?

From her seat in the BMW Tamara catches a glimpse of Cissie, crouched low, zig-zagging her way across the car park towards the club.

Tamara [*Watching Cissie*] Just as well I got it down in shorthand . . .

A preoccupied Henderson replaces the carphone.

Henderson] Hmm?

Boyle's fish truck limps into the car park and conks out alongside the 'covered wagon'.
   Cissie slips into the club as Boyle climbs down from his cab and makes

his way towards Jim Bob's trailer, pulling his jacket on as he goes.
   Tonto emerges from the Winnebago and crosses towards the BMW.
   Boyle and Tonto pass each other.
   Boyle hirples on a few paces, then freezes, one arm in the air, his jacket half-on. He turns.

Boyle] Ho!

Billie and Jolene, their faces up against the microphone onstage, harmonise the last line of their song.

Billie and Jolene [*Singing*] ' . . . just out of reach of these two empty arms . . .'

Billie] Ooooow!

Jolene] Sorry, was that your toe?

Frank glances up from the Dobro frets.

Frank] Ha, look who's here . . .

Cissie makes her way towards the stage.

Cissie [*To hair stylist*] 'Scuse me.

The McPhail Sisters and Friend wind down, Billie and Jolene exchanging 'bodychecks'.
   There is a pitiful smattering of applause from the assembled few.

Frank [*To Cissie*] . . . you just missed my big solo.

Out in the car park a frustrated Fraser Boyle is left clutching on to Frank's Burberry as the white BMW roars away, tyres screaming.

A straggle of cowboys and cowgirls returning from the nearby pub give Boyle a wide berth as he wallops the raincoat on the tarmac in fury.

Cissie is standing in front of the stage engaged in a secretive conversation with Frank who is crouching in front of her.

Cissie [*Sotto voce, to Frank*] C'mon, hurry up, he's goin' to catch his death out there!

Frank] What about me? I'm supposed to stroll about in ma underpants an' a pair of cowboy boots?

Cissie] Don't be daft, he needs the boots as well . . .

She makes a grab for Frank's foot.

Frank] Ho, chuck that!

Just offstage in the corridor Billie and Jolene continue their argument.

Billie] What was I supposed to do, go out there an' tell the world that you were in the huff?

Jolene] I was not in the huff, I was incommunicado!

Billie] You were in the bloody closet, Jolene!

Jim Bob and the Wild Bunch file past them on their way onstage.

Jolene] That's right, tell the entire . . .

Billie] Shh.

Jolene] Don't shh me, ya wee . . .

Billie] Shhhh!

Jolene] What?

Billie nods in the direction of the stage where Cissie is standing by the microphone.

Cissie [*Sings*] ' . . . the world looks small and green and the snow-capped mountains white . . . From a distance the ocean meets the stream . . .'

Frank stands with his back to the audience filling in on bottleneck, while Jim Bob and the band pick up on the number.

Cissie stands at the mike, Jim Bob's guitar slung around her neck.

Frank [*To Jim Bob*] If I suddenly gallop offstage it's nothin' personal.

A hapless Fraser Boyle stands at the back of the club, silently cursing, as

155

*the cowboys and cowgirls resume
their seats after the drinks interval.*

*Billie and Jolene wander back
onstage to fill out the sound on guitar,
accordion, and voices.*

*Dorwood hunkers down beside
Tamara's car listening to the distant
music. He glances up at the rumbling
DC10 in the night sky above him. He
shivers.*

*Libo Ragazzo chucks his leather
bag into the stretch limo
parked outside the 'Arrivals'
lounge at Glasgow airport.
He climbs in after it. The car pulls
away smoothly.*

*A young woman in glasses
is sitting next to Ragazzo.
She glances up from some
documents she's going through.*

Young woman in glasses
[*In Italian*] Been a lotta
changes since you left . . .

*Libo Ragazzo stares out
through the window at
the passing city.*

Ragazzo] Mm . . .
Young woman in glasses
[*In Italian*] . . . don't forget
you've to phone Detroit
before . . . [*She glances*

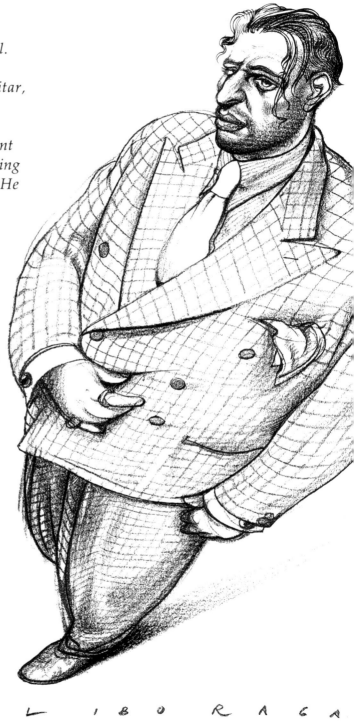

L I B O   R A G A

156

at watch] . . . Signor Ragazzo?

Ragazzo] Huh?

He turns his head.

Young woman in glasses [*In Italian*] Detroit . . . you've to telephone before . . .

Ragazzo [*Interrupting*] Si, grazie.

Young woman in glasses] Prego.

She returns to her documents.

Ragazzo [*After some moments, in Glaswegian*] Bung annurra big Bell's in there, honeybunch.

He holds out his tumbler in a gold-ringed mitt.

    A little while later the limo pulls up at the front of the Holiday Inn.

The McPhail Sisters and Friends are belting out 'From a Distance' from the stage of the Ponderosa.
Outside in the car park Dorwood turns up his jacket collar and wraps his arms around his shivering body.
    By now Tonto has got into the back seat of the BMW and has his head between his knees. He is going

through his hair with his hand.
    Tamara leans forward to Henderson.

Tamara] Ralph, there's something you're not telling me.

Inside the club Cissie and the McPhail Sisters and the Wild Bunch and Friend build towards the climax of 'From a Distance', with Jolene and Cissie harmonising on vocals.
    There is a momentary pause at the end of the song.
    Then the cowboys and cowgirls in the audience are on their feet, whooping and hollering.
    Suddenly, a loud bang is heard from outside the club. The applause dies quickly, and heads in the audience turn away to look.
    In the confusion Cissie slings Jim Bob's guitar around her back and feels about in her shirt for the revolver.

Cissie] Aaaaaaaaaaagh . . .

Outside in the moonlight the navy Colt snags in Dorwood's fingers as it falls to the ground.

- J O L E N E -

The Last Round Up

'Ragazzo's' pokey hat, perched atop the roof of the Bar-L, has a jagged hole in the front, from which a single naked bulb winks weakly.

There is stoned laughter and whoops of delight from the dark as the burglar alarm dies away and the light bulb goes out.

In the street below the white BMW turns the corner and moves along towards the bar.

Tamara MacAskill sits in the back seat as far away from Tonto as she can get, her face buried in her hands.

The Deadwood Playboys' version of 'Hello, Mary Lou' plays on the car radio.

Tonto leans forward, taps Henderson on the shoulder, and points through the windscreen.

Henderson looks, and sees a man swaying on the street corner ahead, a brown paper-wrapped parcel in his hand dribbling its contents on to the pavement.

Tamara] Ralph, will you please tell me what's going on . . . who are these people?

In the car park of the Ponderosa a circle of concerned and curious cowboys and cowgirls huddle around the radio car.

In the middle of the circle are the Tall Cowpoke, Roxanne and Drew. The Tall Cowpoke holds his hand to his ear and blood trickles between his fingers.

Roxanne] Chuck pullin' faces, it's only a crease.

Tall Cowpoke] Crease? A hauf-inch closer an' that wis me . . . brains blootered aw err the tarmac.

Roxanne] It's a car park, no' an erradrome. [*To Drew*] Away an' ask the bouncer fur some ointment.

Drew] You no' be better knottin' a tourniquet roon his froat, naw?

Roxanne] Jist get us the ointment, Drew.

Tall Cowpoke] It's a bullet wound, no' a midgie bite. [*To Drew*] Ask him furra big gless a firewatter, it's goupin' somethin' chronic, tell him.

Drew slopes off.
   A voice rises behind the onlookers.

Boyle] 'Scuse me, pal . . . out ma road . . . 'scuse me . . .

Fraser Boyle forces his way through the crowd.

Boyle] . . . boy made his escape in a motor . . . y'awright?

Roxanne] Efter they vol-a-vongs? Yur jokin'.

Boyle] I'm talkin' to Timberwolf.

Roxanne] *He* didnae huv any vol-a-vongs. Scram.

She pushes Boyle aside and applies a 'kerchief to the Tall Cowpoke's injured ear.

Tall Cowpoke] Watch ma herr.

Boyle [*To Roxanne*] I wouldnae go buyin' him too many stereo albums for his Christmas, sweetheart.

Frank is at the wheel of the radio car speeding away from the Ponderosa. Cissie is sitting next to him peeling the shirt off him as he drives.

Cissie [*Over shoulder*] I'm goin' to murder you . . . what'd you go an' take a pot-shot at that guy for?

Dorwood] It wasnae meant to be a pot-shot . . .

Dorwood is lying on the back seat pulling up his Wranglers.

Dorwood] . . . it was meant to even up the score for aw they hammer hold-ups.

Cissie] I thought you'd killed yourself!

Frank] No such joy.

Dorwood [*To Cissie*] You've got a lotta explainin' to do . . .

Cissie] Like what?

She thrusts the top half of Dorwood's prison pyjamas at Frank. The carphone starts ringing.

Dorwood] . . . like, who is this idiot, an' how come he's wearin' aw ma stuff!

Frank] Somebody better answer that.

Also speeding away from the Ponderosa, Jim Bob's Winnebago has taken the Aberdeen road. A taxi appears a little way behind them, with Billie and Jolene inside.

Jolene] Did you get a load of the

beanpole? Bang! She was out that door like her tail was on fire . . . nosey big get.

Jolene is changing in the back seat.

Jolene] I havenae seen anybody shift that quick since our Jinty got a call-back for the Coatbridge panto.

Billie] She wasnae too bad a singer, mind you.

Jolene] Yeh, I know, but she was a good head an' shoulders bigger than all the other six dwarfs . . . the boy MacIndoo's sister was playin' Snow White . . . you ever seen a Snow White wi' a stookie leg an' a poncho?

Billie] I'm not talkin' about your Jinty, I'm talkin' about Cissie what's-her-name.

Jolene] Crouch.

Billie] Eh?

Jolene] Crouch . . . her name's Crouch. Don't tell me you didnae tumble?

Billie] Tumble? You don't mean . . .?

Jolene] They've got a four-year-old kid, for God's sake . . .

Billie] . . . the bastard.

Jolene] . . . what'd I do wi' that coat hanger?

Suddenly the taxi comes to a juddering halt.

Jolene] Woh!

In the hotel suite at the Holiday Inn Libo Ragazzo is pacing to and fro with a telephone in his hand and the receiver clamped to his ear. He is wearing a bathrobe, and his hair is still wet. The bedside radio is playing Billie and Jolene's version of 'Quicksilver'.

Ragazzo [*Into phone*] Naw, person to person . . . an' make it snappy, it's nearly six o'clock.

He crosses to the window and peeks out.
    He glances at his wristwatch.

Ragazzo [*Into phone, angrily*] Detroit time, I'm talkin' . . . hurry up.

He gives his wrist a shake, and holds his watch to his free ear.

Ragazzo [*Into phone*] Hullo?

Billie and Jolene's singing fades over the radio.

Radio DJ] The McFabulous McPhail Sisters there with yet another track from our Radio Kelvin *Country Comes to Calton* compilation CD . . . six and a half minutes to eke out before the Midnight News on Kelvinly casual 289.

With the phone still clamped to his

ear Ragazzo crosses to the TV set, he prods the 'on' button with his big toe, and flicks through the channels. He pauses to stare fixedly at the mute re-run of a Deadwood Playboys 'Your Cheatin' Heart' video extract which is followed by a newsreader mouthing to the camera.

He checks his watch again.

Radio DJ] . . . let me just confirm that time check for you . . . it's coming up to seven . . . no, eight . . . eight and a half minutes past twelve . . .

Ragazzo [*Agitated*] C'mon, for God's sake . . . [*Into phone*] . . . hullo!

Radio DJ . . . a gentle reminder that you're tuned to the top-rated . . .

There is an abortive news jingle on the radio.

Radio DJ] . . . in the West . . . Dunky Chisholm standing in for Ward Ferguson in the Midnight Newsroom, and we kick off with a bit of excitement down at the old Rancho Ponderosa tonight, and I don't just mean Jim Bob O'May's one and only Central Scotland appearance before . . . and I'm told that we have made contact with the radio car . . .

Ragazzo [*Into phone*] Hullo?

Radio DJ [*To radio car*] . . . Hullo, Tamara?

Ragazzo [*Into phone*] Is that you, Phil?

Frank [*Into carphone, over radio*] Aw naw, it's that clown off the wireless . . .

Ragazzo [*Into phone*] Naw, it's me . . . Libo.

Radio DJ [*To radio car*] Is that you, Brian?

Frank [*Into carphone, over radio*] Hullo? You're through to . . .

There is a burst of static over the radio.

Ragazzo [*Into phone*] Libo Ragazzo, d'you want me to talk up . . . hullo?

Radio DJ [*To radio car, over static*] I'm sorry, I can't hear you . . .

Frank [*Into carphone, over radio*] . . . but if you'd like to leave a message please speak after the tone.

Ragazzo [*Into phone*] I wish I could, but I'm in Glesca . . .

Frank [*Into carphone, over radio*] Thank you.

Frank whistles a tone into the carphone.

Radio DJ [*To radio car, overlapping whistle*] Could you ask Tamara to fill us in about this latest shooting incident down there in Wishaw?

Ragazzo [*Into phone*] . . . naw, Glesca . . . G-l-a-s-g-o-w.

Radio DJ [*To radio car*] I believe that one of the Wild Bunch may've lost an eye, how accurate is that report . . . hullo?

Ragazzo [*Into phone*] . . . I'm here to pick up that stuff you were inquirin' about.

Frank [*Into carphone, over radio, distant*] Ohyah!

There is a clunk over the radio as the carphone is hung up.

Radio DJ] Hullo?

Ragazzo [*Into phone*] Naw, naw, absolutely no problems on that score, Phil, just to let you know I'll be back in Flowerdale Sunday night . . .

Radio DJ [*To radio car*] Is that Tamara?

Ragazzo [*Into phone*] . . . naw, Sunday.

There is a knock at Ragazzo's hotel room door.

Radio DJ [*Off-mike*] We've lost them, Kathy.

There's another knock at the door.

Ragazzo [*Into phone*] Can you hold on a second, there's somebody . . . [*Loudly*] . . . who is it? I'm on the phone! [*Into phone*] You still there, Phil?

Radio DJ] Hullo?

Ragazzo [*Into phone*] Yeh, I know I promised, but . . .

Ragazzo hears a muffled voice from outside the door.

Muffled Voice] Room Service, that's yur sangwidge order.

Ragazzo [*Into phone*] . . . naw, c'mon, hey, listen, I've still got most of that dough in Detroit, all you have to do is call ma wife an' she'll . . .

There is a sudden crash and a splintering noise as the hotel room door comes crashing down into the room. Ragazzo whips round in a fury.

Ragazzo] . . . I told you I was on the fff . . . [*breaks off*] . . . wait a minute, you urnae Room Serv . . . what you doin'?

Radio DJ] Okay, if there's anybody still awake down there in Wishaw and you happen to've been at tonight's historic Jim Bob gig . . .

Ragazzo [*Shouting*] What you doin'! Naw, don't . . . woyah.

Radio DJ] . . . why not give us a call on Freephone, 0800 . . .

Ragazzo's body slumps on to the floor, the telephone with it.

Telephone Receiver [*Distant*] Ciao, Ragazzo.

As Tonto stands over Ragazzo's

crumpled body a hypodermic syringe falls from his hand and oozes its vile contents on to the carpet. Ragazzo gurgles weakly.

Radio DJ] . . . 775.

The radio car sits outside the New Pancake Roadhouse diner in an otherwise deserted parking lot. The radio is playing.

Radio DJ] . . . 772. A *Country comes to Calton* CD to the first phone-in eyewitness to get through to the *Crime Beat* studio before we go off the air at 2 o'clock. Seven, sorry, nine minutes after midnight . . . Ward Ferguson, if we can find him, with the *Weather Outlook* for ranch-hands in the Glasgow area after this one from . . .

Frank reaches forward to snap the radio off before sinking out of sight in the driver's seat.

Inside the Pancake House Cissie squeezes ten pence into the jukebox, while Dorwood perches on a stool at the counter, scanning the large overhead pancake menu.
  Dorwood is dressed in clothes

previously worn by Frank (including boots). On his head he wears an improvised hat fashioned from a radio Kelvin Country comes to Calton *plastic bag. He has borrowed Frank's Ray-bans.*
  Cissie presses the 'select' button on the jukebox and a Scottish country danceband version of 'Your Cheatin' Heart' *comes up.*
  Cissie crosses to the window overlooking the car park.

Dorwood [*Still scanning menu*] If that's supposed to get ma goat, it doesnae. [*Loudly*] How's about some service out here . . . ho!

He bangs on the counter with a sugar dispenser.
  Cissie stands at the window, her eyes closed.
  Shirley, a pac-a-mac over her waitressing outfit, struggles up the road towards the diner, lugging a large pail of pancake mix. She stops under a streetlight, puts the pail down and looks at the front page of the late edition of the Evening Echo. *She scans the report about Dorwood's escape from custody. Accompanying the report are two photographs: one straightforward mug shot, the other a snap showing Dorwood's head wound.*
  Shirley screws up her face in disgust as she crosses the parking lot.

Cissie disappears from the window. Dorwood swings round from the counter to face the door as Shirley enters.

Dorwood] No' before time.

Shirley gives the jukebox a kick in passing. Its volume drops.

Dorwood] How does yur Three Egg Pancake Special come?

Shirley] Wi' three eggs an' a pancake.

She crosses the room, slings the Echo *on the counter-top, dumps the pail, and removes her pac-a-mac.*

Shirley] What's your companion after?

She nods towards a figure sitting in the corner, the Radio Kelvin 'hat' pulled low over her eyes.

Dorwood] Lemme ask.

He swivels round to face Cissie.

Dorwood] D'you want a coffee?

Shirley] Aw, my God, what happened to your . . .

She breaks off. Her eyes dart to the Evening Echo *on the counter.*

Dorwood] Make that one Special an' two coffees.

He swivels round to face Shirley.

Shirley] Sure . . . lemme . . . er . . . lemme check out back an' see if the hens've laid any . . . er . . .

She edges away from the counter and gropes for the back door handle.

Shirley] . . . any pancakes.

Shirley edges out of the back door of the diner and rushes around the side of the building.

She gallops past the radio car in the car park and heads for a telephone box some hundred yards further up the road.

Frank hears her footsteps and sits bolt upright in the driver's seat. He casts around, eyes unfocused.

He sees Cissie come bursting through the front door of the diner, Dorwood behind her. She hauls the passenger door open and stuffs Dorwood inside.

Frank [*Groggily*] Okay, where's ma pancake?

Cissie] Move!

She chucks the car keys at Frank and jumps in beside him.

Dorwood [*To Frank*] You heard . . . move.

The radio car roars into life, reverses out on to the road, and bucks off in the same direction taken by the galloping Shirley.

Frank] That is a very fetching chapeau . . . all you need is a pair of polythene pantaloons an' . . . hey, is that not what's-her-features from the Bar-L?

The car slows down as it comes level with a flagging Shirley.

Frank] D'you want me to stop an' give her a . . .

There is a smacking noise.

Frank] . . . ohyah!

The car accelerates away, leaving an exhausted Shirley to catch her breath by the roadside.

Billie's taxi is parked at the side of the road in darkness. Billie leans against the taxi wing and scuffs her toe along the ground. Jolene leans out of the passenger door, lights two cigarettes and offers one to Billie.

Jolene] I still am your best pal, I wouldn't 've told you if I didnae think you knew awready . . . I thought you knew awready . . . you sure you didnae know awready?

Jolene puffs on both cigarettes.

Jolene] Everybody else we know knew awready.

Billie] Yeh, thanks.

Jolene] Aw, c'mon, it could be an awful lot worse, at least you're not . . .

Billie stops scuffing and looks up.

Jolene] . . .aw, naw, don't tell me.

Billie] Don't you start, it was an accident!

Jolene] Aw, my God in Heaven, when did this happen?

Billie [*Interrupting*] Mind your own business.

She stomps off up the road.

Jolene It is ma business, I'm your best . . . where you off to?

Billie carries on walking.

Jolene] Come back here.

Billie gets swallowed up in the darkness.

Jolene] Billie?

Jolene steps on to the road and chucks the cigarettes away.
An owl hoots.

Jolene] Billie!

Billie [*In distance*] What?

Jolene] You forgot the can for the diesel.

She holds up a jerry can.

From a deserted approach road there is a distant view of Aberdeen, icily silvered by the dawn creeping up over the sea.

The silence is gradually eroded by a low hornet-like hum that grows into a throaty rumble. A line of motorbikes appears over the horizon like so many Indians in a 'B' western.

Riding at the head of the extended 'V' formation flanking Jim Bob's Winnebago, is a squat man astride a massive Harley Davidson, in aviators and a peaked cap, the studs embedded in the back of his sawn-off scrotum-hide jacket identifying him as 'The Toad'.

The Toad's obvious role model is the young Brando of The Wild One *fame.*

Behind 'The Toad' come the rest of the Loons O'Lucifer [Buchan Chapter] as they ride into the granite city limits.

Fraser Boyle's fish van, coming at the oil capital from a different direction, brakes violently at the crossroads, despite the green light, as the line of bikers cross in front of it.

Boyle sits behind the wheel and stares balefully as a seemingly endless procession of bikers pass in front of the van windscreen.

Cherokee George] Whit you stoppin' fur? Yur lights're at green.

Boyle stops chewing and turns his head.

Cherokee George sits hunched up in the passenger seat. He is wearing Frank's Burberry and still sports the black eye doled out to him in Glasgow.

Cherokee George] Jist plough through the bastarts . . . Too late, yur lights've went tae . . .

The fish van takes off across the junction, narrowly avoiding a collision with a newspaper truck travelling in the opposite direction to the convoy and assiduously following traffic-light instructions to proceed.

Horns blare.

Cherokee George] . . .that's right, get the pairy us kilt!

A bundle of newspapers thump down on to the doorstep of an Aberdeen seafront café.

There, on the front page of the Aberdeen Press & Journal, *is the headline: 'MAFIA BAGMAN FOUND SLAIN IN SCOTTISH HOTEL'. A large photograph of the dead Libo Ragazzo in his bathrobe*

167

accompanies the news item. There is a smaller picture of a hypodermic needle 'similar to the one found at the scene of the crime'.

In the listings box to the right of the page is the info: 'Former North Sea Diver sought in Grampian Region – see page 4'.

Frank, in prison-issue pyjamas, Dorwood's cowboy boots on his feet, and wearing a hospital blanket poncho, plucks a newspaper from the bundle as the delivery boy reboards his truck heading off along the promenade.

Frank flicks through the Press & Journal *pages.*

He looks at a smiling picture of Dorwood in a cowboy hat. The headline above the picture reads: 'Pancake waitress Shirley: "I Was Petrified".'

Frank's lips move silently as he reads the article.

There is a hum as a milk float approaches.

Frank's lips stop moving. He leafs quickly back to the front page.

Frank [*To himself*] Jeesus . . .

On the front page the dead Ragazzo wears a curiously peaceful expression on his bloated face.

The milkman crosses the pavement with a crate of yoghurts and deposits it on the café doorstep. He picks up

the empty crate and re-crosses to his float.

He dumps the empty crate in the back of the float, picks up a crate of milk shakes, and repeats the journey, pausing on the way back to peer over Frank's shoulder at the front page of the newspaper.

Milkman] Quine next door till us has the perfect double o' that dressin' gown, onnly in reid.

He goes back to the float, chucks the second empty crate in to the back, and climbs aboard.

Frank shivers, folds the newspaper, and crosses to the crates of yoghurt and milk shakes.

In a narrow backstreet lane in Aberdeen dockland a young police constable is standing by the now abandoned radio car.

He is reeling off the car number plate into his personal radio.

Police Constable [*Into radio*] Echo, six, one, niner, Tango . . . Foxtrot . . . Jitterbug . . .

Boyle's fish van appears at the far end of the narrow lane and drives down it towards the radio car and the policeman. The young constable steps out on to the cobbles to examine the radio car driver's door.

Boyle brakes sharply some twenty yards away and reverses speedily all the way back up the street.

Police Constable [*Into radio*] . . . no sign of forced entry, over.

There is a blurred response from HQ over the radio.

Boyle's van reaches the top of the narrow street, backs round the corner out of sight, and reappears a few seconds later crossing the gap.

The carphone inside the radio car starts to ring. The young police constable peers in through the window.

Ralph Henderson sits at the wheel of his white BMW, driving through the outskirts of Aberdeen, carphone to his ear.

Henderson] Tammy?

He holds the phone out to a white-faced Tamara sitting beside him.

Tamara stares straight ahead.

Henderson [*Replacing carphone*] Tell you what, why don't I take you to that little French place this evening? Chappie hails from Provence . . . serves up a passable *bourride* by all . . .

Tamara makes a grab for the carphone.

Henderson] . . . uh, uh.
Tamara] Ooow.
Henderson [*Sweetly*] You don't imagine I'm going to let you talk to anyone, do you?

Frank makes his way along the deserted seafront promenade towards a distant beach shelter. His arms are loaded with milk shake and yoghurt cartons.

A growing rumble causes him to turn his head and look behind him.

Cissie sits shivering with her back against the beach shelter, the Dobro case on the bench on one side of her and Dorwood stretched out on the other, his head in her lap. The Winnebago and its biker escort pass behind the shelter.

First one, then several, empty milk shake cartons come sailing over top of the shelter roof.

Dorwood stirs slightly, his stockinged feet rubbing together.

The convoy passes along the promenade towards the fairground site.

Frank appears round the side of the shelter, two yoghurt cartons in his hand.

Frank] Hi, how's the boy?
Cissie] Still asleep, what kept you!

169

Dorwood lets out a moan.

Frank] Loons O'Lucifer had the milk shakes, I'm afraid.

He sits down on the bench at Dorwood's feet and passes a yoghurt carton to Cissie.

Frank] I'll've the turnip one.
Cissie] Did you manage to get a newspaper?

She examines her yoghurt label.

Frank] Yeh . . . boy Ragazzo's dead.

He peels the top off his carton and dips his tongue into the yoghurt.
Dorwood lets out another moan.

Frank] There's a bit about hubby on page 4.

He produces the Press & Journal *from under his poncho.*
Cissie grabs the paper and leafs through it.

Frank] It's not really turnip, it's turnip an' raisin.

He upends the yoghurt down his throat.

Cissie [*Reading*] The rotten pig, I always knew she was a clipe.

Frank] You know I love you, don't you? Who's a clipe?
Cissie] Shirley . . . she phoned the cops right enough . . . they know we're here.

Frank] Naw, they don't . . . it says 'Sought in Grampian Region', that could be anywhere within a radius of . . . ho, wake up . . . [*He gives Dorwood a dunt*] . . . how big is 'Grampian Region'?

Dorwood comes to with a start.

Dorwood [*Groggily*] Wha . . . ?
Cissie [*Sotto voce, to Frank*] What're you doin'!
Dorwood [*Non compos mentis*] Where am I?
Frank] Grampian Region, cops're after you.

He takes the yoghurt carton from Cissie and spoons a dollop into his mouth with his fingers.

Cissie [*Clapping Dorwood on the back*] It's okay, you were asleep.

She shoots Frank a filthy look.

Frank] Bleagh!

He spits a mouthful of yoghurt on to the ground.

Dorwood [*To Cissie*] What you done wi' ma boots?
Frank [*To Cissie*] You might've warned me it was banana!

Cissie [*To Dorwood*] He's got them.

She hides the newspaper behind her back.

Frank [*To Cissie*] An' you've got the cheek to talk about Shirley bein' a clipe? [*To Dorwood*] I was only wearin' them to go for . . . [*pointedly at Cissie*] . . . the newspaper.

He hands the banana yoghurt to Dorwood.

Dorwood] What's this?

Dorwood peers at the carton.

Frank [*To Cissie*] Gonnae get that for us?

He holds a leg out.

Dorwood] Ho, what's he doin' wi' ma boots? [*To Cissie*] Eh? What's he doin' wi' ma boots on!

Cissie] God spare me from all this.

She buries her face in her hands.

Frank [*To Cissie*] I'm not surprised you want a divorce, does he have to say everthin' twice over?

Dorwood] Divorce? What's he talkin' about, divorce! [*To Frank*] What're you talkin' about, divorce!

Frank] Correction . . . thrice over.

Dorwood [*To Cissie*] I thought you told me this guy was brought in by the Samaritans to keep you off the booze?

Frank looks up from tugging at Dorwood's boots.

Cissie [*Through fingers, to Frank*] I had to tell him somethin'.

Dorwood] What've you been sayin' to him?

He chucks the yoghurt carton away and grabs Cissie.

Cissie] Aaargh!

Dorwood] What've you been tellin' this geek about our private business!

Cissie] Chuck that!

Frank] Ho!

He prods Dorwood in the back.

Dorwood] What!

Frank] There's no call to add to this mess.

He points to the litter on the floor.

Dorwood] Listen, ya . . .

He lets go of Cissie and rounds on Frank. Cissie gives him a shove, forcing him to wade through the yoghurt puddle in his bedsocks.

Dorwood] . . . aw, naw!

He stares down at his claggy feet.

Frank] Here, lemme give you these boots.

*Jim Bob's Winnebago and the attendant
Loons O'Lucifer have come to rest by
the Aberdeen beach pavilion. A Loons
O'Lucifer motorcycle 'Guard of
Honour' has been lined up, leading to
Jim Bob's trailer door.*

*The Toad slowly dismounts from
his machine and removes his sawn-off
scrotum-hide jacket. Standing there in
his sleeveless black T-shirt, one cannot
help but be struck by the bold tattoo
on the Toad's beefy bicep. Though not
exactly alike in every detail, the
tattoo is strikingly similar
to the one that Frank
will carry on his
upper arm to
the grave.*

*A Lieutenant moves forward with
sheets of tissue paper and a bottle of
'Ferguzade'. The Toad folds his
colours and places them reverentially
between the sheets of tissue paper.*

*The Toad has a slug of 'Ferguzade'
and he and his Lieutenant move
forward between the two rows of
bikes. The Loon nearest the trailer
door gives it a respectful tap with the
toe of his jackboot.*

*There is the low murmur of
expectant Loons.*

*Fraser Boyle's fish van pulls up
unnoticed and parks nearby. The
Toad adjusts his aviators and gives his
peaked Brando cap a little
twitch. Inside the van
Boyle lights a half-
cigarette and
passes it to
Cherokee
George.*

Cherokee George] D'you see whit I see?

He presses his nose against the windscreen.

Boyle] I don't want to see what you see, I havenae been at the meths, ole buddy.

Cherokee George] Naw, oan the boy's airm . . . it's the dead spit of the wan I done fur that pal a Dwane's the other day there.

Boyle] What pal a Dwane's?

Cherokee George] Big glaikit-luckin' sod, turnt up out the blue in a raincoat no' aw that dissimilar tae . . .

He breaks off and examines the Burberry he's wearing.

Cherokee George] . . . haud oan, where'd you say you bought this?

The Toad reappears at Jim Bob's trailer door and raises a triumphant forearm.

Cherokee George] . . . awyah!

The fish van takes off suddenly and weaves its way past the beach pavilion, just clipping the Toad's mighty Harley in passing. The big machine teeters on its stand. The Toad stops dead in his tracks.

All heads turn and an unearthly hush descends as the Toad's beloved sickle crashes in slow motion to the concrete.

There is a collective gasp of incredulous Loons as the fish van drives unconcernedly off along the promenade.

Jolene sits on one of the fold-down seats of the taxi, her back to Billie. She's strumming Billie's guitar.

Jolene [*Sings*] 'I cry myself to sleep each night an' wish that I could hold you tight . . . ma life's so empty since you went away . . .' [*Breaks off, to Billie*] You thought up any names yet? [*Sings*] 'The pillow that I dream upon . . . ' [*Breaks off*] Rudy's quite nice. [*Sings*] ' . . . is stained with tears since you've been gone' [*Breaks off*] Or there's Randy? [*Sings*] 'An' it keeps right on a . . . ' [*Breaks off*] Naw, scrub Randy, you don't want any crass individuals passin' remarks . . . [*Sings*] ' . . . hurtin' since you've . . .'

The taxi comes to a juddering stop.

Jolene [*Breaks off*] What you stoppin' for?

Later that afternoon Frank and Cissie are seated in a stationary Waltzer bucket on the carnival site.

> *The afternoon light is fading and, except for the occasional Loon passing in the middle distance, the site is deserted.*

Frank] So?
Cissie] So what?

Frank removes his prison-issue pyjama top and slips an arm into the sleeve of Cissie's jacket.

Frank] So what? I told you I loved you, didn't I?

He gropes behind his back without success for the other sleeve.

Cissie] Look, I'm only lendin' you a jacket, for God's sake.
Frank [*Interrupting*] Naw, back in that beach bunker, you pretended not to hear me.

The 'Eagle of the Apocalypse' on Frank's upper arm has healed and lends his otherwise spindly limbs a certain macho credibility.

Cissie] I was readin' my yoghurt.

The Toad makes his way around the Waltzer towards them.

Frank] Aw, yeh?
The Toad] Ho!
Cissie] I don't think we should be here.

She makes to get up. Frank breaks off groping for the other sleeve and takes hold of her arm.

Frank] Sit where you are.

The Toad draws level with their bucket.

Frank] So what's with the 'Ho', Jim?

He turns to face the Toad.

The Toad] 'Hojim'?
Frank] You're just after shoutin' 'Ho!', I trust that wasnae at us? [*Aside, to Cissie*] You might've told me he was built like a bus shelter!

The Toad peers at Frank's tattoo, then at his own.

Frank] We were just goin', it was her that wanted to sit here.

He starts getting up.

Cissie] It was not!
The Toad] Nae sweat, min . . .

He presses Frank back into his seat.

The Toad] . . . I didna ken ye wur a Loon, ken?
Frank] Yeh, right. [*To Cissie*] What's a 'Loonken'?
The Toad [*Leering over Cissie*] Fit Chapter ye wi'?
Cissie [*To Frank*] You tell him.
Frank] Chapter? Aw . . . er . . . The Devil-dogs . . . Carfin.

174

Cissie [*To The Toad*] Chuck oglin' us.

The Toad [*To Frank*] Fit'd she say?

Frank [*Apologetically*] I think it's your after-shave. [*Sotto voce, to Cissie*] D'you want us to die?

The Toad] Ho!

He leans forward and pokes Frank.

The Toad [*Close to Frank's face*] S'nae a bad-lookin' quinie . . . if I ever loss the errial aff me sickle I'll ken far tae come till.

He winks and swings off along the Waltzer.

Cissie] What'd he say?

Frank] Biker talk . . .

He locates the missing sleeve and sticks his arm down it.

Cissie] D'you not feel stupit in that?

Frank] What . . . this?

Cissie] Accordin' to Dorwood it buttons up the wrong side.

Frank] Accordin' to Dorwood the entire planet buttons up the wrong side . . . has he always been that narky?

Cissie] You'd be that narky if you'd got seven years for somethin' you didn't do.

She gets up to go.

Frank] You don't still believe that nonsense, do you?

Cissie] Of course I believe it, I'm married to him, amn't I?

Frank] You could put a tune to that an' sell it to Tammy Wynette . . . naw, wait, don't go. Cissie!

He grabs her arm.

Cissie] Leggo ma arm, I've got to go an' hunt for . . .

Frank pulls her close.

Cissie] . . . what you doin'?

Frank leans forward and kisses her tenderly on the lips.
He breaks away and looks at her for some response.
She regards him balefully.

Frank] Well?

Cissie [*Shaking her head*] Nup . . . sorry.

Frank] Awright . . . c'mere.

He takes her in his arms and presses his lips to hers, and they sink down into the bucket locked in an embrace.
Suddenly the lights around them come on as the Waltzer comes to life. A husky steam organ version of 'Your Cheatin' Heart' begins to play as the waltzer buckets start to move.
The volume of the music swells.
In the control booth of the waltzer the Toad, oilcan in hand, is tinkering with the speed and volume controls as Frank and Cissie spin past him.

The Waltzer whirls round at breakneck speed and still Frank and Cissie embrace. Cissie's hair corkscrews behind her as the lights shed a rainbow across her cheek.

Slowly, the Waltzer begins to slacken its reckless pace, and the steam organ starts to run out of puff. The bucket begins to rotate at a more leisurely speed, and the lights start going out one by one.

The Waltzer finally grinds to a halt where it started.

Cissie sits there, eyes shut, knuckles white on the handlebar as the steam organ wheezes out a final grace note.

Frank looks at Cissie. Then looks away.

Cissie slowly opens her eyelids.

Cissie [*Softly*] Wow.

Dorwood stands on the seashore at the water's edge, the incoming tide lapping over his one cowboy boot and one bedsock. He stares out to sea and steels himself against the icy spume carried on the evening breeze.

A supply vessel battles through the waves on her way out to the far-off rigs.

Dorwood looks down at the revolver and checks the chamber.

Two slugs left.

Cherokee George and Fraser Boyle are sitting in the fish van on the edge of the carnival site eating fish and chips out of newspaper.

Cherokee George has a fresh black eye to keep the other one company.

Cherokee George] You want tae know somethin'?

Boyle stares through the windscreen as one or two fathers and small sons wander forlornly between the boarded-up stall and sideshows. The Loons o' Lucifer, in contrast, cluster around Snowy's mobile fish, chip and coffee stall which sits in a pool of light on a patch of ground vacated by the showman's caravan.

Boyle] Naw, but I can tell from the way you're munchin' that you're gonnae to add to ma aready bulgin' catalogue of totally useless information.

Cherokee George scrunches up his chip paper, smacks his lips, and wipes his hands down the Burberry.

Cherokee George] That hus tae be the worst fish supper I've ever hud in ma life.

Boyle] Didnae deter you from molocatin' it, I notice.

Cherokee George] It wis me that bought them . . . d'you want a beverage?

He opens the van door.

Boyle] Aye, get us a hot choclit . . . an' listen . . . don't you go an' do a bunk, that stuff's up here someplace an' I'm gonnae need a good buddy to give us a hand to get it off the get that's got it an' get it to Jim Bob afore he gets on that boat the morra, get me?

Cherokee George weighs this up for several seconds.

Cherokee George] What happens if they don't huv any hot choclit?

On another part of the carnival site Frank and Cissie meander between the boarded-up booths, Frank's arm around Cissie's shoulder, hers around his waist.

Frank] If that gets too heavy gimme a shout an' we'll dump it.

Cissie is lugging the Dobro case. She looks at Frank.

Frank] What?
Cissie] Nothin' . . . I'm just tryin' to picture what you were like as a toddler.

She leans her head on his shoulder.

Frank] Much as I am the now . . . totally irresist . . . aw, naw.

He stops dead.

Frank] Is this Friday?
Cissie] I think so . . . why?
Frank] I forgot to phone in ma copy.
Cissie] Copy?
Frank] For the 'Rab Haw' column. What time d'you make it?
Cissie] What you goin' to phone in? You havenae eaten anythin' all day.

She turns her gaze upwards to the sky and Frank joins her in staring upwards.
    A blanket of twinkling stars covers the heavens.

Frank] I had a turnip yoghurt at breakfast time.
Cissie] Turnip an' raisin.
Frank] I just need to find myself a telephone . . .
Cissie] Look!

A shooting star traverses the velvet black sky and burns itself out.

Frank [*Looking down and around*] Where?
Cissie] That means you can make a wish.
Frank] Aw . . . I thought you'd spotted a phonebox.

Cissie stands with her head tilted back, and her eyes shut now.

Frank] Cissie?

She lowers her gaze and looks at Frank.

Frank [*Swallows*] God, see when you look at me like that, you put all thoughts of turnips an' raisins right out of ma head.

He leans forward and kisses her.
Cissie drops the Dobro case on to Frank's foot (the one without the cowboy boot on) and puts her arms around him.

Frank [*Softly*] Ohyah.

Cissie leans forward and kisses Frank.

Frank] 'Know how it slipped ma mind?

He picks up the Dobro case and puts his arm around Cissie.
They walk on.

Frank] I wasnae wearin' ma Rab Haw rain . . .

He breaks off as he sees Cherokee George stroll between the booths up ahead wearing Frank's Burberry and looking exactly like Dopey from the Seven Dwarves.

Frank] . . . coat.

He looks at Cissie. Cissie looks at him. They both look at the now-empty gap between the booths.
Frank drops the Dobro case and breaks into a lop-sided trot.
Up ahead Cherokee George picks his way between the parked motorbikes by Snowy's stall to get to the counter.
He squeezes himself between some lounging Loons and slaps a couple of coins down.

Cherokee George] Wan coffee, wan choclit, baith hot.

Snowy, the lugubrious stallholder, carries on wiping the counter-top with a filthy cloth.

Cherokee George] You want tae get a big sign up there . . . 'The Worst Fish Suppers in Scotland, Bar None'.

He looks around at the assembled Loons, failing to notice that they are all happily munching on Snowy's renowned fish suppers.

Cherokee George [*To Loons*] I've scoffed a few fish suppers in ma time an' I don't mind tellin' youse people, that wis the worst fish supper I ever hud in ma life.

The Loons stop munching.

Cherokee George] Naw, straight up,

178

it hus tae be the worst fish supper I ever hud in ma life. Seriously.

He turns back to Snowy.

Cherokee George] Bung a coupla broon sugars in the choclit, will you, Chief? S'fur the boy in the fish motor.

He turns once more to the Loons.

Cherokee George] Goat tae keep the bastart sweet, eh?

Frank is peering round the corner of Snowy's stall and watching the commotion. Cissie stands behind him.

Frank [*Over shoulder*] 'Course I want it back but this may not be the most opportune . . .

Cherokee George] Waaaaaaaaaaagh!

Cissie [*Distressed*] Can you not go an' help him?

She leans over the top of Frank and tries peering round the corner.

Frank [*Straightening up*] Help him? That's the guy that landed me wi' this!

He taps his tattooed arm.

Cissie] Cherokee George? What's he doin' in Aberdeen?

There is a sudden roar from a mighty Harley Davidson.

Cherokee George] Aaaaaaaaaaaaaa- aaaaaaaaaaaaaargh!

The Toad roars through the gap between booths with Cherokee George roped by his ankles to the back of his bike, getting dragged along the ground in Frank's Burberry.

Frank [*Laughing*] There's your answer. [*Stops laughing*] Hey, ma good coat!

★ ★ ★

Billie and Jolene are cruising along the Aberdeen promenade in the taxi. Jolene is sitting up in the back seat.

Jolene] Aw, look, Billie, the Shows!

She presses her nose against the window.

Billie [*Over shoulder*] Yeh, an' they're shut.

Jolene] So, they're shut? Still the Shows, innit? God, you're that crabbit, gettin'.

They hear the roar of the Harley as the Toad circles the showground in search of the fish van.

Cherokee George] Waaaaaaaaaa- aaaaaaaaaaaaaaaaaooooooooh!

Jolene] See that? Somebody's enjoyin' theirself.

She sticks her tongue out at the back of Billie's head.

Frank and Cissie stand in a shop doorway across from a row of terraced houses.

Frank] It's got nothin' to do with it bein' a 'security blanket' . . . it's a very practical garment.

Cissie stares across the road at a lighted second-floor window.

Frank] I had my furst crab curry in that coat.

Cissie carries on staring.

Frank] Ma furst serious hangover.

Cissie cranes forward.

Frank] Ma furst bout of food poisonin' . . . my last crab curry . . .
Cissie] C'mon.

She suddenly takes off along the street, walking fast.
Frank breaks into a run to catch her.

Frank] . . . you not wantin' to wait an' catch a glimpse of him, naw?

Cissie strides along, one hand to her face.

Cissie] He'll be in his bed.

As their backs are turned away a woman appears at the lighted window and reaches up to draw the curtains. She pauses and stoops down and gathers up a four-year-old boy in her arms. The boy laughs as they draw the other half of the curtains shut.

Cissie [*Distant*] I just wanted to make sure he was happy, that was all.

The white BMW is parked discreetly not far away from the beach pavilion and Jim Bob's Winnebago.

Henderson] 'Fraid we'll have to take a raincheck on that *bourride*, sweetie . . . don't think you're quite up to it, hmm?

Tamara is slumped in the back seat. She looks like she's dead, but her eyes are open and she is still breathing . . . just.
Henderson picks up the carphone.

Henderson] Believe me, the people who were eliminated were scum, Tammy . . .

He punches in a number.

Henderson] . . . the sort you write about in that little newspaper of yours. [*Into phone*] Hi, we spoke last night, I'm in a position to deliver.

He reaches behind him and adjusts Tamara's collar.

Henderson [*Into phone*] . . . no, not quite that much . . . about six, seven kilos . . . all right . . . six . . . listen, I can just as easily . . . [*Listens*] . . . wise fellow.

He replaces the receiver.

Henderson] Back in a jiffy, darling . . . don't go 'way, you hear?

He reaches out and touches Tamara's cold cheek. He smiles.
Henderson gets out of the car and goes around to the boot. He turns the key and throws the boot-lid open. He reaches in, removes a parcel, and reaches up to close the lid.
A revolver barrel glints in the moonlight and Henderson freezes as the gun is placed just behind his ear.

Dorwood] Nice an' easy does it.

Henderson closes the boot-lid nice and easily.

Dorwood] Right, start walkin'.

Henderson steps away from the car.

Dorwood] Slow! Walk slow, I've only got the one boot.

He brings the gun down and jabs it into Henderson's back, forcing him forward towards the roadway traversing their path to Jim Bob's trailer.

Dorwood] I just hope she's gonnae be okay in that motor, or that's three murders that're gonnae appear on the charge sheet alongside whatever else you've been . . . get that down!

He knocks Henderson's upraised right arm down to his side.

Dorwood] D'you want everybody to know I've got a gun at your back?
Henderson [*Over shoulder*] So you tell me . . . I've only got your word for . . .
Dorwood [*Interrupting*] Try me.

Dorwood cocks the gun.
Henderson arrives at the kerb and stops.

Dorwood] What you waitin' for, the lollipop man?

He prods Henderson in the back with the revolver. But Henderson stays put.

Henderson] I've just wet myself.
Dorwood] So, you get scurvy legs . . . walk, I said!

Billie's taxi is approaching the beach pavilion. Jolene scrunches up her fish supper paper.

Jolene] God, that was scrumptious, how was yours?

Billie leans forward and peers through the windscreen. Through it she sees Henderson and Dorwood cross the road in front of them.

Jolene] I don't recall our Jinty goin' deaf when she fell pregnant. Hoi, I'm talkin' to you, McPhail.

Billie slows down and turns around to Jolene.

Billie] You're never gonnae believe this, Jolene, but guess who I've just seen!

She turns back to look through the windscreen again.
  The road ahead is now completely deserted.

Jolene] Wasnae the boy MacIndoo, was it?

The taxi shrieks to a halt and Billie leaps out.
  She stands looking around her in the headlight beams.

Jolene] Wee Desmond, naw?

Jolene makes to get out of the taxi.

Billie] I swear to God, Jolene . . .

Jolene] Don't be ridiculous, Billie, what would Dorwood be doin' up in Aberdeen?

She rushes up to Billie.

Jolene] He's just after fallin' off a roof in Glas . . . [*Stops*]

Billie turns to face her.

Billie] He's just after what?

Dorwood holds the revolver against Henderson's temple as they press themselves against Jim Bob's trailer in the dark near the beach pavilion.

Approaching the cliff-edge Fraser Boyle sees a crumpled coat on the ground. He gathers up the tattered Burberry and inches closer through the moonlight to the cliff edge.

Boyle] Hullo! Y'err, George?

Below him, on the rocky beach, Boyle can see his van sitting on its nose, rear doors agape.

Boyle [*Shouting down*] George? [*Loudly*] Ur you down there, ya dozy half-breed!

He can hear the waves crashing on the distant beach below.

Boyle [*To himself*] Ach, I give up . . .

He turns away and starts walking.

Cherokee George [*Distant*] I still think that wis the worst fish supper I ever hud in ma life!

Boyle stops, turns, and heads back to the cliff-edge.

Back in town a police patrol car cruises along the seafront promenade. An indecipherable message can be heard over the car radio, the single intelligible word of which is an 'over' at the end.
As the police car's tail lights disappear along the promenade, Frank and Cissie emerge from their hiding place.

Frank] We could always go to the nearest bingo hall an' get the manager to flash a message up on the screen . . . 'Will Dorwood Crouch, last seen wearing one cowboy boot . . .'

They pass the discreetly parked white BMW. Frank stops by the driver's door.

Cissie] I wish I could remember what pubs we used to . . . [*Breaks off*] . . . come away from there!

Frank] Be with you in a second . . .

He tries the handle and the door opens.

Frank] . . . I just want to make a quick phonecall to ma Features Editor.

Onstage inside the beach pavilion Jim Bob O'May and the Wild Bunch are brewing up a storm.

Jim Bob [*Sings*] 'Well, I never felt more like singing the blues . . .'

There is the sound of an exultant roar from the assembled Loons o' Lucifer.

Jim Bob] ' . . . 'cos I never thought that I'd ever lose your love, dear . . .'

Loon bops with Loon in the aisles.

Jim Bob [*Sings*] ' . . . why'd you leave me this way . . .'

Jim Bob and the Wild Bunch give the classic early 50s' hit big licks from the beach pavilion stage.
Few of the bopping Loons pay much heed to the pedal-steel player, who keeps somewhat out of the limelight under his stetson, or to the fact that he is wearing only one cowboy boot under his pedal-steel guitar table.

*Frank has climbed inside the white
BMW and is speaking on the
carphone.*

Frank] . . . aw, an' listen, could you
ask one of the paramedics to bring
us somethin' to eat . . . anythin' but
yoghurt . . . we're starvin' . . .
thanks.

*He replaces the phone and leans out
of the open door.*

Frank] Be here in two minutes, how
is she?

*Cissie and Tamara, acting like a
bendi-toy, are walking to and fro
beside the car.
    They hear a police whoop-whoop
nearby.*

Cissie] You can see how she is . . . if
we hadn't found her she'd've
snuffed it . . . [*To Tamara*] . . .
C'mon, walk, dammit!

*Frank climbs out of the car and goes
over to them. He examines an ugly
bruise on the inside of Tamara's
forearm with a tiny red puncture
mark at its centre.*

Frank] D'you suppose this's self-
inflicted or . . .

*He breaks off as the police car whoop-
whoop approaches.*

Frank] . . . oh, oh, that's me then.

*He raises his arms above his head and
walks to meet the oncoming red,
white, and blue flashing lights.*

Cissie] Where the hell d'you think
you're goin'!
Frank [*Over shoulder*] It's okay, Hank
Fonda got off when they found out
it was a case of mistaken . . .

*The patrol car speeds straight past
him and on towards Jim Bob's trailer.*

Frank] . . . identity.

*A disgruntled Frank lowers his
upraised arms, he looks across
towards the trailer.*

Cissie] Hoi, quit sulkin' an' come an'
help me with her!

*An Aberdeen matron with a small dog
on a lead stands in the beach pavilion
parking lot a few yards distant, as two
police patrol officers bend over
Henderson's body.
    One of his officers turns Henderson
on to his back. Henderson's face is a
white powdery mask.*

First Patrol Officer] He's nae been

out for his Hallowe'en, has he?

The matron's dog starts yapping.

Matron] Quiet, Monty!
Second Patrol Officer [*Into personal radio*] Y'there, HQ, over?

Inside the pavilion Jim Bob and Jolene are sharing the vocals, leading the Wild Bunch through a rockin' Country version of the Bellamy Brothers' 'Let Your Love Flow'.

Backstage in the dressing room Billie stands staring into the mirror, her face cupped in her hands. Jim Bob and Jolene's duetting voices are playing over the tannoy.

Billie [*In answer to song*] Yeh, sure, no problem!

Her head drops on to the dressing table top.

Jim Bob and Jolene combine in joyous harmony over the tannoy.

Some flashing blue lights pass the dressing room window as two ambulances speed Tamara and Henderson to hospital.

Further down the beach, away from the pavilion, Cissie and Frank sit a few feet apart on a beach shelter bench.

Frank runs his fingers over the Dobro strings as a wintery sun claws its way up the beach. He eases awkwardly into a slide-guitar version of 'Your Cheatin' Heart'.

Out in the distant sea, a Norwegian ferryboat forges its way towards the far horizon.

The sun has now risen and Cissie's hair looks burnished by its light. The Dobro lies beside its case on the bench.

Frank is gone.

Frank is at the wheel of a taxi, speeding out of Aberdeen on the way to Glasgow.

Billie and Jolene are asleep in the back amid a pile of clothes, amps, guitars and other clutter.

Frank notices a man slumped by the roadside ahead of the taxi.

As the car approaches a dishevelled looking Fraser Boyle stands up, holding out a tattered raincoat with the word 'Glesca' daubed across the back.

Frank [*To himself*] Yeh, some hope.

He gives a laugh as the taxi sails past Boyle.

Frank [*Laugh dies*] Ho, wait a minute, that was ma Burberry!

He turns to look back, and sees Boyle's diminishing figure behind him.

Cissie stands in front of the beach shelter looking out to sea.

Walking behind the shelter, along the promenade, is a woman hand in hand with a small boy about four years old.

As the boy and the woman pass along the promenade, Cissie picks up the Dobro case, quits the beach shelter and heads off along the beach in the opposite direction.

Beside one of her footprints in the sand there is a brief glimpse of gunmetal as the sun catches on the navy Colt revolver.

Cissie walks on.

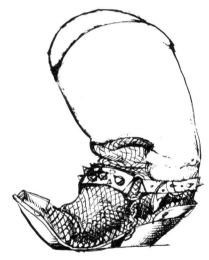